GETTING LUCKY

ANNIE J. ROSE

CHAPTER 1

CHRIS

Summer in Chicago was especially miserable in the afternoon, but the cold air in Paddy's Art Emporium made it bearable. Thankfully, with nothing else on my schedule for the evening, I could take my time in my favorite art supply store.

I was forever on a mission for the perfect paintbrush. And that didn't just mean durability and non-shedding, all-natural versus synthetic fibers, but affordability as well. As any artist knew, they could get expensive, and well, I was tough on my brushes.

I didn't pay any mind to the front counter when I entered the store and headed to the back on my mission. I had the bad habit of keeping my head down and minding my own business, unlike some people in the city, but mostly, I was ready to get in and out. And since I knew Paddy's like the back of my hand, I didn't need any help.

"Sable. Ox hair. Here we go—synthetic." I grabbed a brush off the display and checked the end for bounce. "Nope. Not good enough. Seventeen fifty? I don't think so."

I mumbled to myself, checking out the thickness of the fibers, making sure they went across the entire width of the brush, and that if the tips were supposed to be round, they were round, flat needed to be flat, and fans had better have a fan.

Sure, I had my usual brands and styles—the staples, as I called them—but now that opportunity was in the air, I wanted to flex my muscles a bit and see if I could add something new to my arsenal.

I was one of the lucky ones, and I knew it. Unlike so many, I'd been fortunate enough to have an art dealer find me after my senior year, and now I had a blank white wall with my name on. It was ready for something new. Something marvelous.

I just had to find the subject. I wanted something edgy to match my style, but I also wanted to play with colors I never had before.

I took a small round-tip brush from the display and checked the quality. "You. You're going home with me, beautiful."

"I beg your pardon?" a small voice from behind me answered.

I spun around to find a riot of color surrounding the most beautiful pair of eyes I'd ever seen. Like a kaleidoscope, they were a mixture of bright green and blue, and the tiny flecks of gold made a starburst pattern that played with the fluorescents above.

Her short-cropped hot pink hair, just a shade lighter than magenta, only added to the rainbow.

"I'm sorry. I was talking about the brush," I said. I held it up to show her. "It's perfect."

"Oh," she said. "Do you always talk to your brushes?" It was only then I realized she had on one of Paddy's lime-green smocks and a box tucked under her arm, and she was putting out some new paint tubes in the aisle behind me. "Or flirt with them, I guess I should say."

My face warmed, and I wondered if it had turned as pink as her hair. "Um, not as a habit, but—okay, maybe at times. You know, to boost their self-esteem a little. Happy brushes make happy paintings. Or at least I think that's what Bob Ross said."

She smiled, and it was like the clouds parting to reveal the sunshine just after an instance of rain. "It's cool. I see all kinds come in here. Artists and their flair. I can dig it." She gave me a wink and then turned around to finish her task.

She had really snuck up on me. "You say that like you're not one of us," I said, assuming anyone who worked at Paddy's would have to be at least vaguely interested in art. Or at least crafting.

"I'm not."

"You're *not* an artist? Crafter? Do you doodle?" I found that hard to believe with her style.

"No, but I do take art classes in college."

I couldn't help but chuckle. The girl was obviously pulling my leg. "Good one."

She gave me the side-eye. "I'm serious. I mean, I like art, and color, obviously, but I'm not really good at it. I only took the class to piss off my father."

"I'm intrigued. My name is Chris, by the way. I've never seen you in here before. Did you just start?"

"I'm Hope, and yes. I've been here for about three days now. Something else I've done to piss off my father." She seemed rather proud of that fact.

"Did it work?"

She angled toward me and took a bow. "And for my next trick."

A girl with daddy issues? I tried not to be so dirty-minded and went back to my task.

She finished putting the tubes on their pegs and then crushed the little box they'd come out of. "If you need anything, Chris, I'll be at the counter. But then again, you could probably give *me* a lesson on this place. So, keep that in mind."

As she walked away, I laughed, thinking of exactly what kind of lesson I'd like to give her. But I had to get my mind wrapped around my art and not how sexy she was.

I went ahead and turned to the other side of the aisle where she had apparently just stocked the raw umber. The tubes were crammed on the peg, and a few colors were evenly balanced on top like I'd never seen. I found a few of the bright colors I wanted to try, found a replacement or two for the colors I'd used up, and then grabbed a huge jar of gesso, which would help me prepare my canvas for painting.

Since my hands were full, and I never subjected myself to the indignity of carrying a handbasket, even though it was the smart thing to do, so I decided it was time to stop spending and proceeded to the checkout.

Hope was standing behind the counter, reading a pamphlet. "Here's a coupon for ten percent off on your next purchase if you want it." She pushed the paper across the counter as I dumped all of my stuff on top of it.

"I'll take it. Thanks." I glanced down and realized it was for the particular brand of paint I'd chosen. "You look like you've already gotten the hang of things."

"I'm a business major. I hope I can handle being a clerk." She rang up each item and bagged them as she went. Then she carefully wrapped my paintbrushes together in tissue paper, per Paddy's rules, and placed them in the bag as if they were made of glass.

"You know I'm just going to beat the hell out of those when I get them home, right?"

"Ah, well, here at Paddy's, we leave the abuse to the artists. My manager says always wrap the brushes and be careful with all pencils. Something about the leads breaking." She shrugged. "I don't have to understand it; I just have to do it. I'm pretty sure there's a method to the madness."

I chuckled. I liked her sense of humor, and she was so pretty, looking like an enchanted pixie from a fairy tale, that I couldn't stop looking at her.

"That's going to be sixty-eight dollars and forty-six cents."

I passed her my card. "Not bad."

"Assuming you found everything you need," she said.

"And then some. But the good news is, if I have to come back, I'll get another visit with you." I gave her my best-winning smile as she finished the transaction and passed me a slip to sign.

"I look forward to your next visit, Chris." Her smile looked a bit devilish, and I couldn't help but think of what it would be like to kiss that pouty mouth of hers. Her lips were nice and full, the kind I could find countless uses for.

"Thanks," I said, taking my receipt and giving her the signed copy. "Maybe I'll see you around."

"If you're lucky."

I left still trying to focus on one of my many ideas.

Since I lived above a tattoo parlor, in a building that my mother owned, I had endless inspiration if I had in mind doing another series that would reflect the lifestyle.

I had many tats myself, so most of my work featured tattooed youth and the cultural influences surrounding my generation. But now, I just wanted to make something different. Something fresh. It was the dream of all artists, and a feat rarely pulled off. Mostly everything was a regurgitated idea from the past, even if done unintentionally. Because there was truly nothing new under the sun.

I arrived at my building and went inside the tattoo parlor, where my roommate, Puck, was working on a client. He had been sleeping on my sofa off and on since college—even though he managed a successful business, I liked his company, so I didn't really mind him hanging around. One good thing about it, he was never late to work, and since I knew where he lived, he was never late paying the rent.

"How's it going?" he asked. "Did you ever find some inspiration?"

Inspiration usually found me, striking me in the head like it wouldn't be ignored, or coming to me when I least expected it. But it was something I had never been able to force. "I'm still waiting on it to find me," I said, taking to the stairs. "I'm going to order takeout if you want to place an order."

"I'm good, man. I just need to finish up Taylor here, and I have a six-hour session tonight."

"Don't break your back. You're going to be hurting tomorrow when that fat wallet has you sitting lopsided."

Puck laughed, scratching his beard as he glanced up at me from his dark-rimmed glasses. "I'd rather have a sore back than be broke, my brother."

"I hear ya." I walked up, and when I hit the landing, I took out my keys. Puck usually kept the door to the house locked so that none of the customers could wander up and enter our apartment, and today was no exception.

Once I fished out the keys, I opened the door and went to the couch, where I placed the bag of supplies on the coffee table.

I went through the new merchandise, taking out the pack of brushes. I was still lost on what to do, so I decided to let my mind take me where it wanted to go. Inspiration would either find me or it wouldn't.

I went up to my studio, also known as my loft bedroom, and found my sketchbook and some colored pencils. Then I went to my bed and let the pencil do the walking as my mind drifted.

It wasn't intentional starting off with the color pink, but there was something so refreshing about it. I kept the pencil moving across the paper, and then I found some blue, some green, and a little bit of yellow. Those colors were like a song across the page, singing a specific melody, and I couldn't get enough of the sound.

It was like something possessed me at times. As if some ancient being channeled through me hoping to be heard, my hands the only chance it had to get its point across.

I stayed there for hours, letting the process take over, and when I was done, I tossed the pad aside and then got up to go to the bathroom. After taking a piss and then going down to the kitchen to get a drink, I walked back up to continue.

And when I took the tablet off the bed, glancing down to see my work with fresh eyes, I couldn't get over how close to life I'd drawn her. Hope. The pixie girl with pink hair.

As she stared up at me, it was as if I had just found my life calling, and I knew in an instant that she would be my study. My muse. This would be my masterpiece, the focus from where all others in the series were born.

I quickly went back to work on it, coming up with a few different concepts and hoping the inspiration that had struck wouldn't fade away before I had a chance to get all of my ideas down on paper.

I couldn't believe how true to life I could get from memory alone, and once I had the concepts down, I was ready to break out the paints.

I worked like a feverish madman well into the night, even after Puck got home from his long session. Then I worked until I couldn't keep my eyes open any longer and stepped away from the painting with all intention of waking up and starting right back at it again.

As I crawled into my bed with paint-smudged fingers, I turned over, hugged my pillow, and stared at my pixie girl on the canvas across the room until I fell asleep.

CHAPTER 2

HOPE

The next morning, I hurried into art class and found my place at the back of the room. I had barely made it to class on time, and since I wasn't at all interested in most of what the professor had to say, I spent the hour trying to force myself to focus on his lecture.

After he stopped a moment to rest his voice and take a swig of coffee, which he practically gargled, he turned back to the class. "Could someone tell me where mummy brown gets its name?" Professor Simon's question got my full attention.

I hadn't thought he was going to give a pop quiz, or I might have tried harder, and to my dismay, it was me he called upon for his answer. "Miss Mayhew? Let's see if all of that yawning you've done for the past hour affected your hearing."

"I'm sorry, what was the color? Mummy brown?"

"Yes, mummy brown." He looked down his horn-rimmed glasses, which usually made him less threatening.

"Um, from mummies?" I had hoped to get a few laughs, but no one batted an eye. Not one giggle.

"Could you be more specific?"

"You mean it's really made from mummies?" I crinkled my nose and made a face. "Like actual dead guys?"

Professor Simon sighed. "Mr. Cornwell, would you like to answer?"

Chet Cornwell, who looked more like a dumb jock than an artist, smirked at me before answering, "Mummy brown is made from the ground-up remains from the mummies of ancient pharaohs."

"That is correct. And can anyone tell me the bleak history from what Indian yellow was made?"

A few people made disgusted faces. "Come on. I know it's horrible, but you might see it on a test somewhere." Hands were going up all around the room, and I felt like she was the only one in the class who hadn't been paying attention.

I would never look at paint the same way again. I also decided that maybe art was a bit more interesting than I thought it would be. I just hadn't ever really given it a try.

My father had always considered artists slackers, and I was always discouraged from drawing or painting, even as a child. The only time I had was during elementary art through high school, and even then, he preferred I take any other elective besides art.

At twenty-four, I definitely had more control over what I did with my time. And somehow Chris made me want to be a bit more interested.

"Miss Mayhew, I'd like you to see you at my desk. Everyone else, you're dismissed."

I had never been called out in such a way, and I felt like I could slip down in my seat and disappear into the cracks between the floor tiles. Instead, I got up and walked to his desk, where I awaited his presence.

He walked over after all the others had left. "Now, Miss Mayhew. Did you know that I can tell when you're listening and when your mind is somewhere else?"

"I'm sorry. It's just that I don't really know anything about art. I guess I thought it would be something that interested me more."

"Well, it's too late to switch classes, and honestly, you're not the worst student I have. I just need you to focus. Listen to the lectures, glean what you can, and then when you get a chance to draw, do your best. It's fine if it's just a grade, but at least make the most of your time. You're here anyway. You might as well."

"Yes, sir."

"The next time I call on you, I want you to be prepared."

"I will be."

Professor Simon gave me a hopeful look and then turned around to push his chair in. "You're dismissed. I'll see you Wednesday."

I left the class wondering how long a tube of paint would last. I couldn't tell the professor that, at the moment, my only interest in art was the artist, and his name was Chris. I hadn't stopped thinking about him since he left the store, and I couldn't wait to see him again. I knew it was ridiculous to get so hung up on a customer, but he was so sexy, his dirty blonde hair cropped shorter than my own, and those eyes. Damn, they were so dreamy.

I found myself getting tingles just thinking about him. It had been many batteries ago since my last encounter with my ex-boyfriend Roland. Chris was way hotter.

"Are you blushing?" a voice asked.

I looked up and realized my best friend, Nicole, was heading right for me. "I'm just feeling a bit flushed. It's nothing, really."

She gave me a look that said she didn't believe me. "That's not nothing. That's hot-guy flush." She looked around us across campus and at the young men on the sidewalk. "Who is he, and where did you meet him?" Nicole had been my best friend since my first day of college, and she was always there to confide in when I needed a friend or someone to dye my hair for me. She could also read me like a book, which was pretty scary at times.

I played it down. "It's silly. There's this artist who came into Paddy's yesterday evening. He was totally gorgeous. He had tattoos all up and down his arms and possibly more along his toned chest. He really brought new meaning to being tall, dark, and handsome, and I can't stop thinking about him."

"You don't just like him because you know it will make your old man crazy? I'd suggest not getting into another relationship to piss him off. You are going to end up getting hurt again." I felt like I always had to defend my last relationship, even though I had actually liked Roland when I met him.

"That's not it. And anyway, I'm sure he didn't even notice me like that." Chris had been really into those brushes.

"If he missed you, he's blind and not worth your time. There would obviously be some deep issues going on with his sanity to miss a beauty like you." Her words warmed my heart. What if he *did* notice? My heart tingled.

"I'm not talking about my hair. Even though this color does tend to slap most people in the face." Nicole had always adored my pink hair, but some people hated it.

"I'm not talking about your hair either. You're a catch. You have a bright future on top of being a knockout. And don't even make me remind you of your rich daddy."

"Ugh, don't bring him into it. This guy doesn't know I have a rich daddy, and besides, I don't ask him for his money. I got a job so I can support myself." I was trying to anyway. Living in Chicago was expensive.

"Living in a house he pays for while you earn a little bit of extra spending cash is hardly being self-sufficient. And that's okay. You should make him support you for all you have to put up with." Her honesty could be brutal, but she always meant well.

"Don't you have somewhere to be?" I asked, still feeling a little bruised by her comments. Nicole always shot it to me straight, but sometimes I got caught in the line of fire.

"Hope don't be mad at me for speaking the truth. You know I love you." She gave me a look as if to plead with me not to hate her.

But how could I? She was only telling me the truth and keeping it real. "I'm not." I gave her a reassuring look. "But I do have to get home. I have a ton of crap to do before work."

"I'll call you later. I want to hear all about this guy, especially if you see him again." She had always wanted every detail of gossip, and I couldn't wait to share it. She knew all of my deepest darkest secrets, and I knew hers.

"There's not much to tell. We talked a little, but mostly about work and art."

"Well, maybe it will turn into something more, like pillow talk," she said, wagging her eyebrows. "If he comes back in, you should give him your number."

"Maybe I will. But you know me, I don't just go jumping into bed with someone on the first date."

"Maybe you should live a little. You're master of your

own domain, and it's not like you'd make it a habit. Besides, maybe a hot, tattooed artist is just what you need. He's got bad boy written all over him." She flashed me one last wink, and then we parted ways.

I crossed campus to the parking lot and approached my car. I got in, locked the doors quickly, then started the car and headed home.

I thought about Chris on the way, and of all the things I might say to him when I saw him again. I didn't even know what kind of art he was into, or his last name for that matter. I would have to get his information if I wanted to find him on social media. But then, maybe he wasn't into that. Maybe he thought I was a snob? *Not liking art? He's an artist. He probably thinks we have nothing in common.*

Before I got home, I had created an entire relationship in my mind. I watched it blossom and fail, then wither and die. Just once, I would like to see something working in my future. But there was always one person who I couldn't ignore. He was always lurking, waiting until the moment he could ruin my life. My father.

After stopping for a bite of late lunch and a little light shopping for the fridge, I arrived at home.

Once I put everything up, I walked into the bedroom, kicked off my shoes, and stripped down naked. I had rushed to school after sleeping late, so when I went into the bathroom, I started a hot shower. I had to get ready to go to work, and hopefully, with any luck, my favorite customer would pay me a visit.

I stepped under the spray in the shower, closing my eyes to imagine him there with me. Then I washed my body, lathering my skin as my hands lingered a little lower than usual, taking a deep breath as the feelings of pleasure consumed me.

Before I knew it, I was caught up in it, kissing him in my mind as I imagined our bodies entwined. It was a lovely dream and served its purpose, but when I opened my eyes, the stark white of the shower tile was like a big dose of reality. I'd never felt so alone. So in need of company.

The warm water washed over me, taking the fantasy down the drain. "Let it go, Hope. Get to work, and if you see him, you see him. He probably doesn't even remember you by now."

After convincing myself that I had enough trouble with men just having my father in my life, I got out, got dressed, and headed to work. I didn't want Jude, my manager, to be upset with me. She had taken a chance on me based solely on my business skills, but I knew if I was late, she'd kick me to the curb faster than I could say splat.

As I drove past the store, I caught a glimpse of him walking down the sidewalk. He had come from Paddy's and had a bag from a purchase. "No!" I shouted as he got into a red car. "Oh, no. I missed him."

I wanted to wither and die right there on the spot, but I still had to find parking and get my ass to work.

By the time I made it into the store, James, my coworker, who was a big, tall guy and a bit on the husky side, was checking out a customer. I waited until the old man was leaving with his large canvas before asking about Chris.

"Hey, did you just check out a guy before him? He had blonde hair and tattoos. It wasn't like ten minutes ago."

His eyes were tired, and I could tell it had been a long day from the dark circles under them. He took off his smock as I stepped behind the counter. "Oh, you mean the dude with the pink paint?"

"Pink paint?" That was a surprise.

"Yeah. It was just like your hair. He had about five big tubes of it."

"Five tubes?" What was he doing with all of that pink?

He let out a long breath of frustration. "Are you going to repeat everything I say? Because I'd really like to go home now."

"Sorry. Um, did he say anything?" Surely, he hadn't come back just to see me. He probably just realized he needed the paint for a flower or something. Maybe he was painting a clown?

"No, he just looked around and bought the paint. He's in here a lot. I'm sure you'll see him again." He walked away, dragging his smock on the floor. I found mine under the counter, where I liked to stash it between shifts, and put it on. It was going to be a long night, but at least I could put all of my delusions and hopes behind me.

CHAPTER 3

I was practically drowning myself in coffee when Puck joined me in the kitchen. After two days of binge painting, I needed to refuel.

"Hey, man, are you going to drink that coffee or make love to it? Because I'll give you a little privacy if you need it."

"It's been another long night, but I think inspiration finally found me. Which is a good thing. I got the entire back wall of the gallery, and it's looking pretty bare at the moment. Virginia is supposed to be popping by later to take a look at my progress. So, don't have anyone's ass hanging out when she comes through."

"I can't promise you that, man, but I'll try and not show her mine." He leaned back against the counter and sipped from his favorite mug. It was white and had a big, black arrow pointing up at his face. In bold letters, it read My Ugly Mug.

"Dude, seriously. She nearly fainted the last time with the piercings. Just do me a favor. She hates coming here anyway." It wasn't that we were in a bad part of town, but it was a tattoo parlor, and Virginia liked to think of herself as more refined than most.

"I'll behave." He held up his hand. "Scout's honor."

"I'm just glad I have something to show her that I'm really proud of."

"That's great, man. But maybe you should shower before she gets here. I know you like to steep in your art, but you're smelling ripe." He waved his hand in front of his nose.

"That's your upper lip," I said, knowing full well he was only teasing. Despite steeping in my art, I had showered. It was the only thing that had kept me awake at 3:00 a.m.

Puck narrowed his eyes and pointed to the big, hot pink streak of paint I'd gotten down my forearm. "I take it you're not going for your usual style?"

"Yeah, I am finally branching out a bit with this series. You know I've wanted to for a while. I like the darker stuff, the wild colors of the tattoo styles in the past, but this, it's going to be good for me." It would be even better if I could manage to see my sexy pixie again.

"Hot pink, though? Are you sure, man? I mean, I think it's a cool color and all, but your stuff is usually vivid in a much different way."

"I think it's going to be great." And maybe someday I could show him the source of inspiration. "And Virginia will be pleasantly surprised. She's been wanting me to do something a bit more striking, and I think this is perfect."

"Well, good luck. I've got a full plate today. I'm meeting with my canvas for Ink Fest."

"Did you go with the girl?"

"Hell yeah. Jules. I think she'll be better for my portfolio. Besides, I couldn't pass up a canvas like that."

"Yeah, if my canvases looked like that, my binges would be much longer."

Puck chuckled. "If she wasn't my best customer's sister, it might be better, but Conrad's already warned me. You should give tattooing another try, my friend."

I thought back to the one time he'd let me tattoo his leg, and how terrible it turned out. Not only that, but I wasn't interested in being that up close and personal with random people. It wasn't like every client you got was a hot girl. "No, I'm done with that. I can't stand a canvas that bleeds. I'm the only one I want bleeding for my art."

"Well, you look like you're bleeding pink paint."

"I'll have to get cleaned up a bit before Virginia gets here." I had hoped I'd be able to get back to work, but there was so much to do with her stopping by the studio.

"I'll buzz you when she's on her way up."

"Thanks, man." I took my coffee to the stairs. It was time to go up and make my bed and clean my studio enough to take it at least to a professional level of filth.

I put the screen up in front of my bed, which was in the corner of the room, tucked in the back like an afterthought, which was exactly how I was feeling about sleep.

After I cleaned, I downed the rest of my coffee, which had gone cold, and then went to the bathroom to freshen up.

Seeing I had a streak of paint on my cheek, mixed in with my stubble, I decided to shower. Virginia shouldn't make it there before I was done.

I went down to the bathroom and made sure to bring a change of clothes just in case she surprised me. It was a good thing, because fifteen minutes later when I was drying off, I could hear Puck's voice as well as Virginia's.

The two were making small talk as they entered the apartment.

"He's been holed up for the past two days working on it. I hope he's really doing something great and not slipping into mental oblivion."

"I'm sure it will be wonderful."

I decided that was my cue to join them and found them on their way up to my studio.

"Ah, Virginia. You're early." She was dressed in a tight skirt and wore a blouse and heels that matched, showing off the fact that, for her age, she had long, toned legs. Her blonde hair was swept up in a tight bun, her scowl like a school teacher. All she needed was a ruler.

"I hoped I'd find you working," she said from the stairs. She gave me a pointed look and then turned to continue up them. Although my hair was still wet, I joined them, but only after running my fingers through it to make sure I'd remembered to get the soap out of it.

"I had to clean up so I can go out for more supplies later." I didn't have to go out for supplies, but she didn't know that.

Once we hit the top of the stairs, I walked around them to get to the painting. I wanted to see her reaction when she saw it. "Here it is," I said. "It's the first of many to come in this series. What do you think?"

Virginia looked a bit surprised, but not in a bad way. She stepped back and turned her head to the side as if chewing on her words a bit before speaking. "I like it. It's a lot bolder than what I'm used to from you, but it's vivid, and yet, there's something about the girl's eyes. It's like she holds some great, dark mystery." She took a few steps to look at it from a different angle. "She's very striking, strong, and powerful. I have to say, she is very much like a female superhero. Very clever of you. Everyone loves powerful women. It's sure to be a hit."

"Yeah, and she's hot," Puck said, earning a glance and an eye roll from Virginia.

"Well, at least everyone will appreciate it for something," she mumbled. She was still a bit hesitant about Puck from the last time they'd met when he was piercing a woman's nipples.

"I like the color choice. The pink hair makes it look like a fantasy. It's like she's looking at us from a different reality."

She was a fantasy all right, but I wasn't going to tell Virginia about her. I was just thankful the woman was pleased.

"So, how many canvases are you going to do? I mean, it's a big wall."

"I've already got it mapped out. There are eighteen in all. Here is the sketch of the idea. Our girl is the focal point, the striking center, and then the other canvases will be placed around her, showing the rest of the street scene behind her. The chaos in the colors, the busy city around her fading off in the distance. I want it to look as if it's three dimensional as if you could walk right into it and take her hand. The canvases will make it look like the image is breaking away as if the audience is just about to lose her."

Virginia looked back up at the painting. "She's beckoning the audience, for sure. And it does add a bit of urgency." She let out a sigh. "I don't know why I worry about you, Chris. You always manage to pull off something amazing. Something that draws a crowd. Now, can you have this done by the end of next week?"

"I'm confident that I can. In fact, I've already got the other canvases prepped, and the sketches are on them. I just have to fill her in with paint and add that special touch of detail."

"Then I guess I should leave you to it," she said. "I'll be ready for you on Thursday evening. We'll get them placed and ready for Friday's crowd." She held out her hand, and I took it, giving it a firm shake.

Virginia glanced at Puck, looking down her nose. "Mr. Puck. It was good to see you again," she said as if it were her duty and not something she really meant.

"Oh, the pleasure was all mine," he said, giving her a wink.

Her expression fell as she walked to the stairs. "I'll show myself out."

Once she was gone, Puck reached out and pushed me. "You dirty dog. Who is that pink-haired hottie? And don't tell me you just made her up."

"I don't know who she is yet, but I plan on finding out."

CHAPTER 4

HOPE

A week later, on my way to Professor Simon's art class, I realized I had all but given up on seeing my hot artist again. If he had been by Paddy's it had occurred when I wasn't there, which told me that, after all that time, he wasn't thinking about me at all, and certainly not as much as I was dreaming about him.

I had become obsessed with him as a fantasy, and while it hurt to think it was all one-sided, at least I'd had that much.

When I got to class, everyone was at their assigned stations, chatting quietly around their easels, and Professor Simon was standing at his desk, drinking from his travel cup.

I walked to my place in the back and put my bag down. Then I took out my supplies and placed them on the small table beside me.

The professor waited until everyone had arrived to begin. "I trust that you've all figured out what you're going to do with your time today. Whether you're still working out your strategy, or transferring your image to the canvas, or you're almost done, like a couple of you overachievers, I want you to use the time in class to your advantage. Time management can be just as important as creativity when it comes to working in the art world. Whether you're working with a private client, or perhaps a gallery."

He walked to the chalkboard, where he usually wrote our daily notes, and began to write. "I'd like for you to take this down," he said. "As I told you at the start of the summer semester, there will be many opportunities to get grades by participation. And this is one of those opportunities. However, unlike *other* opportunities, this one is *not* optional. A very special former student of mine is having his gallery exhibit tomorrow night, and I expect all of you to attend and show him some support. Christian Tate was one of my most gifted students, and he brings techniques and flair that I think you'd all benefit from. That's why I will take no excuses. If you can't make it, you don't get the grade. So, if you have plans, cancel them, or better yet, invite your friends to stop by for a second."

Chet raised his hand. "Do we get extra credit for bringing our friends?"

Professor Simon put his hand to his chin. "Hm. That's a good idea, actually, but no. Show up and pass, don't show, you fail. That should be enough incentive, don't you think?"

The class nodded. A few of the girls were whispering to each other, and from what I could gather, a few of them knew the artist in question's work.

Once again, I was feeling a bit left out of the loop. So, I opened the file on my phone with the photo I was planning to paint and then began sketching it onto the canvas. Thankfully it would be painted over because my eraser wasn't working as good as I needed it to.

Rosa, who sat next to me, leaned over while I was having a meltdown. "Here, try this one. You should really invest in a kneaded eraser. They work so much better on canvas, and you can get the fine line when you need it because you can shape the putty however you want."

"Thanks," I said, taking the little ball of black and gray putty. "I'll have to pick one up at Paddy's."

She smiled. "If I might give you a little more advice?" She leaned in a little closer. "Don't use such a heavy hand on your outline. It's a lot easier to hide and erase if needed. Besides, it's only a guideline, remember?"

"Oh, yeah. Thanks." I had heard something about that at the start of the semester. The whole idea of the outline was to be light. I had forgotten. I wanted to be able to see it.

I used the eraser to pick up a lot of the lines like Rosa showed me, and then I was ready to start filling in things with the paint. I had chosen to do a tree. One half would depict a magical winter night sky while the other would show a budding tree with the sunny spring sky. It looked easy enough and would hit all of the elements Professor Simon had required for the grade.

When class was over, Professor Simon walked over and tapped on the board. "Don't forget to go and see Chris's exhibit. No excuses. He's sent a personal invitation to my classes, so I expect to see you there."

Chris? Could it be the same person?

I left only to run into Nicole again. "What's up, daydreamer. If you keep walking around with your head in the clouds, you're going to end up falling on your face."

"I don't have my head in the clouds. I was just trying to figure something out."

"Oh? Let me guess; it's about that hot art guy?"

"Maybe." I had talked about him too much to her already.

"Look, if he hasn't come back in, then I hate to say it, but he's really not that into you. I mean, like I said before, I think he's crazy for not being into you, but that's his problem."

"It's not that. I mean, yeah, I wish I'd gotten to see him, but Professor Simon was saying that we had to go to an exhibit on Friday for an artist named Chris. I just thought that it might be him."

"Oh, so you're thinking about going?"

"I have to go. It's for a grade, and it's mandatory. But I was told I could bring a friend if you're into it?"

She gave me an apologetic look. "I can't. I'm driving out to my mom's that evening. She's dating some new guy and wants me to meet him. I'd rather poke my eyes out, but I'm trying to humor her."

"Where did she meet this one?" Her mother was always bringing someone home to meet Nicole. And strangely enough, it didn't take long after for trouble to start.

"At her yoga class. He's like seven years younger, and I'm pretty sure he's just looking for a good time. I'm sure I'll put the final nail in that coffin. I seem to have a way with scaring them off."

"That's because you can be a bit domineering."

"Hey, I can't help it. I'm just brutally honest."

"Sometimes, you're just brutal."

"It's a gift," she said with a smile and a shrug. She ran her hands through her long brown hair and then readjusted her purse strap. "Hit me up later if you find out about mystery art guy. I'm anxious to see if you're going to get to see him again."

"Me too. I guess I shouldn't get my hopes up, though. He's not even come back into the store when I'm there. You'd think if he was interested, he would."

"Don't let that get you down. Maybe he's a busy man. He might be the hot rising artist on the scene." She was only getting my hopes up again.

"And he could be painting by numbers in his basement. I'll call you when I figure out which." We parted ways, and I hurried to my car, where I tried to find him on Instagram. Turned out, there were a few Christian Tates, but since I was running late for work, I decided I had better get on the road. I'd have plenty of time to check him out between checking out customers, and there wasn't any use pissing Jude off.

I drove through and got a coffee and a pastry, and then I drove down the street to Paddy's and found a place to park. Every time I passed the place now, I had to look for my sexy artist and was always disappointed when I didn't see him.

I walked in, and after leaving my bag in my locker, I punched in and walked up front to see James talking to Jude. When he saw me, he said his goodbyes and then hurried to the back.

"What's got him in a hurry," I asked Jude.

"He's been waiting for you to get here. He's got a dental appointment."

"I've never seen anyone that excited about getting their teeth drilled." I wasn't even sure that's what he was doing, but then James didn't seem like he let too much faze him.

"He's a strange one."

"Hey, do you know an artist named Christian Tate?"

"Oh, sure. He's in here all the time," she said. "Chris is one of our best customers. I send him coupons at Christmas he buys so much. Why? Did you meet him here?"

"Is he blonde, with tattoos and piercings?"

"That's him. He looks like he'd be a tattoo artist, right? Some of his art is even done in that style."

"So, it *was* him I met," I mumbled. Jude looked a bit confused. "Oh, I was only asking because my professor said that we had to go to his exhibit this Friday night. I have to do it for a grade."

Jude let out a moan of frustration. "I'm so jealous. I wish I was able to go. I have to go on a fishing trip with my husband. Talk about boring. It's a good thing James has the late shift Friday. You will love the exhibit. Chris is an amazing artist. His talent is like no one I've ever seen before. Everything is so true to life; it's like you can just walk right into his paintings."

"I can't wait to see his work," I said. I couldn't believe I was going to get to see him again after all. "Maybe it will inspire me to want to create art as well." I was really beginning to appreciate art in a whole new way now that I was taking classes and meeting gorgeous artists.

"You won't be disappointed." Jude walked away from the counter and to the back, leaving me there all alone at the front of the store as usual.

She usually worked restocking or in the office if she was around, and I didn't mind being in charge of the front because it would mean I'd get to see whoever came in, especially Chris. If and when he ran out of something.

Knowing Jude would be in the back, I decided to call Nicole with the latest news.

"What's up, buttercup?" she said upon answering.

"It's him! The hot artist is the one I'll be seeing this weekend!"

"No way! Girl, you are the luckiest lady in the world. I wish I could go. Damn my mother's relationships."

"It's okay. I'll call you after and tell you how it went. I'm hoping he remembers me."

Nicole laughed. "I'm pretty sure he will. You're a little hard to forget."

I heard footsteps coming from the back, and Jude called out to me. "Hope, we have to find the broom. I don't know where James left it, but there's a mess of glitter in aisle five."

"Hey, I have to go! I'll call you later."

I hated that we didn't have more time to talk, but I wasn't going to get fired and give my father any ammo. He'd already been on my ass about getting a job, and if I embarrassed him by getting fired, I'd never hear the end of it.

I'd just have to anticipate the exhibit alone. Maybe Jude would tell me more about him. I knew one thing: Friday night couldn't come fast enough.

CHAPTER 5

CHRIS

The exhibit had really drawn a crowd, and while I had talked to a lot of different people who all praised my work and congratulated me on my success, including my mother, who had bowed out early to meet with a client, I couldn't stop looking for Hope.

"Oh my God," one girl, who stood in front of the painting, said, "That's Hope, from Professor Simon's class."

"It can't be," another said. "She didn't say anything about it."

"Well, she probably wanted this to be a surprise. And she works at Paddy's, remember?"

Hearing them talk, I hoped I hadn't made a huge mistake. What if she showed up and was mortified to be on display? It wasn't that the art was in poor taste, by any means, but it hadn't occurred to me that this might not go as I had planned.

Professor Simon, who had been a big part of my career taking off, walked over to where I stood with Virginia. "Is that Hope Mayhew?" he asked. "The resemblance is uncanny."

"It is. I met her at the art store. She's a real beauty, don't you agree?" I wondered what he thought of his student. What if they didn't get along?

"She's actually got some promise, but she lacks confidence and passion. I had hoped that my class would be the introduction to art that she needed to really get excited about it. I'm just a little disappointed that she didn't tell me she would be featured here tonight. She never even mentioned it."

"No, sir. She wouldn't have. It was done purely from memory. I only see her at the shop when I go in to buy supplies."

"This is incredible work. She must have really caught your eye." His watch made a sound, and then he looked regretful as he apologized. "I'm sorry, I really have to take this. The wife won't be ignored. Remember that before you say any I dos." He gave a chuckle and then walked away.

I turned around as Virginia locked her arm with mine. "You didn't tell me you used a live model. And without consent?"

"Yeah, well, it just sort of happened." And I had just sort of invited all of her classmates and professor, to make sure that I would see her again.

"Well, let's hope that she doesn't see it and freak out."

About that time, Puck walked up to shake my hand. He winked at Virginia and then took a glass of wine from the passing waiter's tray. "This is amazing, my friend. I couldn't be prouder of you if you were my own brother. Look at this turnout."

Virginia clenched my arm, and just when I thought she was upset about Puck, she took in a large breath.

There was a collective hush across the crowd that was followed by applause.

Hope, who had just walked in wearing a short, tight dress that showed off her curves, stopped and applauded me too. And then I saw it, the moment her eyes found the portrait that took up an entire wall and eighteen different canvases of various sizes.

She put her hand on her heart as the others continued to applaud. Her cheeks flushed, and she looked like she might grow faint as she blinked repeatedly. I realized I should at least walk over to greet her or take a bow or something.

"That's me," she said. "You painted me?"

"I'm sorry. I hope you're not mad."

She seemed to be taking it all in. "Oh, not at all, it's just a bit unexpected—and big."

Puck walked over and held out his hand. "I'm Puck. I knew you had to be real."

Before he could say anything to upset the situation, I decided to step in. "I just met Hope at Paddy's, and inspiration struck. I was intrigued by her."

"For obvious reasons. Might I say you are absolutely gorgeous? Every bit as fine as you are on that canvas, if not more."

Just then, the two girls from her class walked over. "You look great, Hope. But why didn't you tell us you were the featured model? Even Professor Simon was surprised."

"I didn't know anything about it, honestly. Chris here surprised me." Her eyes were filled with amazement, and I could tell she was still a tad overwhelmed.

Finally, after everyone had made their rounds, enjoying not only the beauty of my work, but of my model, and congratulating us both on a job well done, the crowd dwindled, and the room went quiet.

I found her standing close to the wall, looking into the canvas that depicted her perfect face. "Do you like it?"

"I love it," she said. "I'm a little unsure about being the center of attention, though. If I had known, I'd have bought a new dress instead of wearing this old thing."

"You are beautiful, and that dress is amazing, by the way."

"I almost wore jeans," she said, giving me the side-eye over her glass of wine.

"Okay, I'm sorry. I should have given you a heads-up."

"Well, it's not like you knew I'd be here." She paused a moment, and when I looked away, taking a deep breath, she groaned. "Seriously? You invited Professor Simon's class, so I'd show up?"

"You're a very smart girl," I said. "You told me that you took art in college, and since I know Professor Simon on a personal basis, I went to the college, saw that you were on his roster, and then sent the invite." I didn't realize how much I sounded like a stalker until I said it all out loud.

"Wow." She took a sip of her drink. "So, you were thinking about me. Why not just come into Paddy's and tell me you wanted to paint me?"

"I didn't know I wanted to until I got started. You stayed with me, and I found it hard to get you out of my mind. Besides, I went to the store five times and every time you were off."

"I'll have to give you my schedule."

"I'd like that."

She laughed softly. "Well, this is very flattering. I've never had a surprise from a stranger as big as this."

"I don't want to be a stranger, Hope. I'd honestly like to get to know you a lot better."

"Judging from the detail of your memory, you know me pretty well already."

"That's always been a gift. All I have to do is see something that fascinates me, and I'm like a sponge absorbing their image down to the fine details. It only happens once in a while."

"Well, I'll consider myself lucky, I suppose."

"I'm the lucky one." I glanced around and realized that there were a lot less people around. Puck had left to make an appointment earlier in the night, and those who remained were either caterers or Virginia's staff. Even the blonde matriarch of the gallery had disappeared.

"Would you like to get out of here and go someplace where we can talk?" I hoped she wouldn't have other plans.

"How do you know I don't have a boyfriend to get home to?"

"I don't." I shrugged.

She grinned. "Would have served you right if I had shown up with another man."

"I'd be devastated," I said, holding my heart. "I guess I was just taking a chance on you."

"Okay," she said. "So, I guess I should return the favor. Although"—she gestured at the painting— "you do look a little obsessed. You're not going to murder me, are you?"

I slumped with exhaustion. She was never going to let me live it down. "How many times do I have to say I'm sorry? Because I'll say it, over and over. I'm sorry I put you on the hook. Please let me have a chance to make it up to you."

She laughed. "You're too easy. So, where are you

taking me?"

"To my dungeon. I mean, for coffee? You're on your third glass."

She turned it up, placing the empty glass on the nearest table. "Correction, I just finished my third glass."

"Did you drive?"

"Actually, I did. How about you?"

"I did too. So, maybe I should drive your car, and we'll see where we end up. Mine is safe here."

"Sounds like a good idea." She took out her keys and handed them to me.

We walked out to the lot, and she led the way to her car. It was a pretty little red convertible BMW. "A beamer?"

"Yeah, it was my father's, and now it's mine." She didn't seem too interested in it as she got into the passenger seat.

I walked around and slid in beside her. "It's nice."

"Thanks. It's a car. It takes me to classes, work, and home. As long as it runs, I don't really pay attention to anything else."

"Where do you want it to drive you tonight?" I asked. "Any particular place you like to eat?"

"Surprise me? And don't try and get all fancy on me because of the car. I'd rather eat a diner any day of the week."

"Cool. I know just the place, then. If you don't mind food trucks." We would see how down-to-earth she was. If she wasn't as spoiled as her car made her out to be, she'd be down for something served on wheels.

She belted a laugh as I started the car. "Are you kidding? I love a good food truck. What are we having?"

"Well, there are a few trucks in my neighborhood. As well as a nice park where we can eat."

"Do you mean down at the Grind?" She reached down

and slipped off her heels.

"Yeah, have you been?" She didn't look like she was spending too much time down in my neighborhood.

"Are you kidding. Pho King Amazing is to die for. And don't even get me started on Shakes, Rattle, and Rolls. That sauce they call rattlesnake juice is so hot I thought my tongue had melted and slipped down my throat."

"It's my favorite," I said. "Well, next to Taco 'Bout Tasty."

Her eyes lit up. "A man after my own heart. I can't believe you live around there. You must be so lucky to eat that all the time."

"That's good and bad," I said, patting my middle. "But luckily, the gym is right around the corner from the tattoo shop."

"Tattoo shop? Is that where you get your tattoos? They look amazing, by the way."

I was flattered she'd noticed. "Yeah, where I live. Well, I live above it, but I own the building. Puck, the guy at the exhibit, he manages it, and he sleeps on my couch. I can get ink whenever I want it. He's my artist. The only person I trust with my skin."

"That's so cool. He seemed really nice. Is he there now?" she asked, shifting in her seat.

"In the shop, probably. Friday nights are usually busy."

I smiled as I downshifted and hit the highway. I couldn't wait to see what happened next.

CHAPTER 6

HOPE

Chris and I drove across the city and parked in the alley behind his house. Then, we walked a block to the Grind, a small park known for its food trucks and nightclubs.

"I'm getting the sweet bacon bao," he said. "Have you ever tried it?"

"No. I think I want a noodle bowl. Did you want to call your friend and see if he wants anything?"

"He'll have his apprentice pick him something up if he's hungry. And knowing Puck, he isn't going to want to eat this late."

"I can't believe I'm eating this late either. Maybe I should just get a bacon bao too."

"It's good. Trust me."

Strangely, I did trust him, as if I'd known him for weeks instead of just dreaming about him.

We ordered our food and then carried it back up the road with us. I couldn't believe we were going to his house, but I liked his company.

Before we made it back, he turned to me, stopping us in the middle of the road. "You know, if you don't want to eat at my house, we can just eat here. Where it's nice and public. I mean, I don't want you to think I'm trying to get too personal."

"Oh, you mean like studying every detail of my body and painting it from memory?" I gave him a sideward look, and he seemed to deflate. "I'm only teasing. But let's face it, the mystery is gone."

"Hey, I haven't seen you naked." He closed his eyes and shook his head. "That came out wrong."

I couldn't help but laugh. He was a bit nervous, but only that he was going to offend me. "You're really sweet, you know. I mean, aside from your stalker painting habits."

"Ugh," he said, looking dramatic. He continued back toward his home.

"I'm kidding!" I stopped him and went up onto my toes to kiss him. His lips were soft and warm against mine. He deepened the kiss, and our tongues mingled, making my body tingle.

"You don't know how long I've thought about doing that," he whispered as he pulled away.

"The whole time you painted me?" I asked, feeling my face grow as warm as my core.

He nodded. "Yes, and the first moment I laid my eyes on you, I knew you were special."

"I thought about you too," I said, not believing I was admitting it. "I wished I could see you again. And when I went to the gallery tonight, I knew who you were. Jude from work helped me make the connection. I wasn't expecting you to even remember me."

"How could I forget you? I feel like we're kindred spirits in some odd way. Like we were meant to meet."

"I know what you mean. I kept seeing us together for some reason." I looked away, my shoulders sagging as I realized how stupid that must have sounded. "Look at me, getting carried away. I mean, I don't want to make more out of it than you intended. I guess I'm letting the flattery get the best of me."

"No, you're not. I think you're feeling the same thing I am. I feel like I've known you for ages, and not just because I've memorized every inch of your body, even parts I've never seen, but something in me just found you." He kissed me again, then pulled away much too soon.

"We should get back to my place before our food gets cold. We have all the time you want to talk."

I didn't speak; I let the minutes go by thinking about how Nicole had told me to take a chance. But if he was just blowing smoke, and the painting was some elaborate pickup line, I was going to be devastated if I let things go too far. I wanted him; I just didn't want to get hurt.

We went to the tattoo parlor, and when we walked inside, his friend Puck stopped his tattooing to greet us. "Well, if it isn't the artist and his muse," he said. "If you two want the apartment, I'll sleep downstairs." He looked right at me and grinned, but then his smile faded as he looked at Chris. "What?"

"Real nice. We're going up to eat and talk for a while. If you need anything, pretend you live somewhere else."

"I do. Down here. Where I'll be sleeping." He turned and gave me an apologetic look. "I'm sorry. You have to excuse me. I let my mouth run away from me at times."

"By at times, he means all the time."

Puck nodded. "Pretty much."

"Come on, Hope, let's see if these sweet bacon baos are

any good." He stepped aside and let me take the stairs before him, then unlocked the door.

I looked around the apartment. It was big, and a lot nicer than I'd imagined from the outside. It wasn't that it was a dump, just an older building, but it appeared to have been recently updated. "Nice place."

"Thanks," he said. "My mom and I wanted to keep a lot of the exterior charm, keeping with the look of the neighborhood, but inside, I needed something that was modern to suit my needs."

"You do your painting here?"

"I do it upstairs in the loft."

I looked up to see that while the living area had tall ceilings, which gave it a dramatic look, the kitchen and bath had an entire upstairs loft above it. "That's your studio?"

"It's my bedroom. But yeah. I guess I paint more than I sleep there. At least lately."

"And Puck sleeps down here?"

"Yeah, he takes the couch. He's saving up for a place of his own, or so he says, but since he works downstairs and I like his company, I don't mind if he crashes here."

"So, does he have to sleep on the couch downstairs often?" It was my way of finding out if he was a man whore or not.

"If you mean, do I bring home a lot of different women, the answer is no. I mean, I guess we both entertain our fair share, but I haven't been in any sort of relationship in over a year. My mom is kind of like your dad, I guess. She's a little too in my business."

He remembered my problems with my father. "Well, parents can be hard on you when they love you. And if your mom is like my dad, then she loves you an awful lot."

"Awful would be a good word for it. But don't get me

wrong, I love the woman." He sat down on the couch and patted the space next to me, then put his bag on the table and took out our food.

"Sweet bacon bao for you. Sweet bacon bao for me. Do you want any extra sauce?"

"No, I'm good. Thanks."

"Here, eat some of the hot fries. You'll get addicted."

We shared the fries and ate our food, and when he was done, he kicked back and put his arm across the back of the couch.

I took my last bite, finished my drink, and then eased back with him. "That was good."

"Do you still feel tipsy?"

"I wasn't tipsy. Even after three glasses."

"So, if I kissed you again, you wouldn't see it as me trying to take advantage of you?"

"Are you trying to take advantage of me?" I leaned in closer. "Because that would be hard to do when I'm sitting here willing. I mean, it's not a habit or anything, but I feel especially close to you."

"Yeah? Me too. Is that weird?"

"No, weird is painting a secret portrait of me and sharing it with half of Chicago." I couldn't even get the words out without laughing.

He kissed me, and it was just like I had dreamed it would be. I melted against him, prepared to take it anywhere he wanted to go. I was going to let down my guard and live for the moment. *Dammit, Nicole. You're a bad influence.*

I shifted in my seat, angling closer, and before I knew it, he was laying me back. He stopped and sat up. "If this is too fast, I can stop."

I knew it was the time I'd usually cut things off, but

there was something about Chris. "What do you see coming from it?" I had to ask; I couldn't just let it happen like I wanted it to. I had to be responsible.

"You're not getting away from me so easily if that's what you mean. And before you tell me how stalkerish that sounds, let me add that I want to see where we can go, if you want that too."

"So, you'll call me in the morning?"

"What? You think I'm kicking you out? Not a chance. I decided when you showed up tonight; I need to see how far we can take it. You're not like anyone I've ever been with, and that's what I like most about you."

I reached for his shirt and pulled him forward as I leaned back. Our lips moved together, and soon our bodies followed. I wasn't sure how far it would all go, but I could already tell that even though we were going for it, he was taking his time with me.

We kissed for a good several minutes before he made a move for my zipper, and only after I'd reached for his.

"Undress for me," he said, sitting back. I did as he requested as he slipped off his shoes, shirt, and undid his pants.

As I unhooked my bra, he took down his pants, licking his lips as if he wanted a taste of me.

"Lie back." He kissed my lips and hovered over me. Then he moved down my body, planting kisses along my breasts and down my tummy. Then he hooked his fingers into my panties and tugged them down.

"You're so beautiful," he said, kissing me between my legs. His tongue dragged across my clit, bringing me to heightened pleasure.

I arched my back and moaned, and then he reached up and traced my lips with two of his fingers.

I took them into my mouth, sucking them to soften his skin. When I was done, he inserted them into my channel, spreading my folds and teasing my clit with his tongue.

After a minute, he ravaged me with his mouth, lapping at my sex until I whimpered. "That feels so good."

"That's all I want to do is make you feel good." He moved over me, stretching out to kiss me, the taste of me still on his lips.

I reached down and gripped his cock. "What about your pleasure?" I asked. "I'd like to make you feel good too." I stroked his erection up and down, feeling the ridges of his thick shaft, which was damned near intimidating.

"It is my pleasure, I promise you. I've been thinking about this all week."

"Creepy," I said with a giggle. He shook his head, but before he could say anything, I had to let him know the truth. "I'm kidding. I've actually been dreaming about this for a while too."

"Really? How creepy," he said, teasing me.

"Did you touch yourself while you thought about me?"

"Maybe. What about you?" He gave me a sideward look. "What? If you get to ask, I get to ask."

"Fine. I'll answer. I may have touched myself in the shower, thinking about you. It was the first night."

"Mm," he said. "That makes me want you even more."

"Then what are you waiting for? I think we've both waited long enough."

"I couldn't agree more." He centered his cock at my entrance and then looked into my eyes as he penetrated me.

I clenched at first because he was much bigger than I was used to, but then he eased his way inside of me, and I closed my eyes, enjoying the pleasure and hoping everything was what it seemed.

He rocked his hips and slowly fucked me, taking special care to work my G-spot and give my clit the attention it craved. I cried out so loudly when I came, I was sure that Puck could hear me downstairs.

"Fuck, that's hot," he said. "I love making you come on my cock. It feels so good." His dirty talk had my head spinning. Or maybe it was the wine after all. But regardless, I never wanted it to end. I held on to his powerful arms as he thrust hard, and then he gathered me up and carried me up the stairs to his bedroom.

He sat down, laying back so I could take control. I rolled my hips, riding him up and down as I ground my pelvis against his. He had thrust slowly, so I began to bounce in a slow and steady rhythm. He slapped my ass, rubbing the tender spots that made it all feel better. With each lick, I felt a shot of pleasure go through me, and then I found my release again, my orgasm ripping through me as my body quaked, milking his cock until he came deep inside me.

I fell to the bed beside him, and he gathered me up in his arms and kissed my temples and then my shoulder. "Fuck. That was amazing, Hope."

"You are amazing," I said, turning my face up to kiss him.

We lay still, our bodies entwined just as they had been in my fantasies, and soon, I fell fast asleep.

After all of the teasing, I wondered if she would give me hell for taking a snapshot of her beauty in the morning light. Waking up beside her was a nice change. And while I wasn't sure I wanted anything as serious as my last relationship, which had ended nastily, I wanted to spend as much time with her as possible.

As she stirred, rousing from her sleep, her soft expressions of sleepiness had me itching to paint her. "I'm sorry, I just have to do it," I said, rolling over to grab my phone. I turned on the camera as she opened one eye and gave me a groggy glance.

"Is that a camera?"

"Yes, and before you make jokes, let me just say that I'm not trying to be creepy, but I'm working."

She smiled and rolled away from me, putting the pillow over her head. "I still think it's creepy," she said. "You could try asking."

"May I continue?" I said, wondering if she was going to get mad at me for my eagerness. "I've been itching to paint you since I woke up and saw how beautiful you look in the morning light."

"You aren't only creepy, but you're delusional. I know my morning face. It's puffy and gross."

I hated that she was putting herself down. "Don't even. You're so naturally pretty, it should be illegal."

She laughed. "I have hot pink hair, and I'm short."

"You're petite." She had the body of a goddess, the type that artists had longed to paint for centuries. I was the luckiest man on earth for meeting her.

But she didn't agree. "I'm too curvy to be petite."

"Well, you're perfect to me. And I won't take any arguments from you about it. You're going to sit there and take the compliments."

She turned around, making a face. "Paint me like this," she said, before sticking out her tongue.

"You're just being a brat now," I said, knowing she was only teasing me. We shared a laugh, and I moved to kiss her, only to have her pull away.

"I didn't bring my toothbrush."

"I don't care if you didn't." I leaned in and kissed her. She was so hot, I wished I could keep her there, naked in my bed all day, but that wasn't going to work out for either of us.

"I have to get up. I have to go to work soon." She sat up on the edge of the bed and then turned to look at me. "Oh no!" she said, putting her hand on her heart. "I have to take you to your car. You left it at the gallery."

"I can get Puck to take me if you can't. It's not a big deal."

"Are you sure?" She moved closer and looked up into my eyes.

"Yes, I'm positive. It's not a big deal. You can't be late

for Paddy's. I need you there so I can get some perks. You know, like coupons, gift certificates, and maybe a free sample now and then?"

She rolled her eyes, knowing I was joking. "You're impossible. I knew that's why you painted me. You chose me for the benefits, didn't you? All of that free paint and pencils. Next, you'll be pimping me out for canvas, you dirty bastard." She put the covers over her breasts and then got to her feet, still playing dramatically. "I will not be used in such a way! How dare you!"

"You should take up acting," I teased. "Maybe you missed your calling."

"If I had chosen a different path, I wouldn't have met you," she said, stepping closer to where I sat on the edge of the bed. "And I'm glad I did. It's not often a girl meets someone interested in more than her body." She paused. "Hey, wait. You scoundrel!" She giggled as she tried to step away, but I pulled her back to my lap.

We kissed each other with equal passion. "I like this," I said. "It's been a long time since I've met someone who was sexy and had a sense of humor."

"You bring it out of me." She reached up and brushed her fingers through my hair. "Some would say that means we're good together."

"I think they'd be right."

"So, we'll see where this goes?"

"Yeah. Do you want to go out again next week sometime?"

"Yes. Will you text?"

"No," I said, shaking my head. "I'm sorry. I can't text you. It's just not going to work for me."

"Oh?" She gave me a pointed look. "And why not?"

"Because I'm too greedy for that. I mean, honestly, I

might text now and then, at the most. But I'd much rather call you and hear that sexy voice."

She smiled. "I'd like that. As long as you don't start getting too attached." She made a face that made me want to take her over my knee and spank her. "I mean, I do have a life—now that I'm a famous model, I'm sure there will be a lot of gentleman callers."

"Oh. That's how it's going to be. You're going to use me for fame?" I kissed her again, and then she pulled away, letting out a deep sigh.

"You're fun. And now I don't want to go. I seriously could stay here and play like this all day."

I knew exactly how she felt. Things were so natural with us. It could have easily gone a different way with the reveal of the painting, but she was an amazing woman, who had to see that I had only the best intentions by her.

"I like that we get along so well. It's refreshing for a change, you know?"

"Funny," she said. "I was thinking the same thing."

I got up and handed her my robe from across the room. "Here, take this, and you can shower here. Your clothes are still downstairs with mine." As I stood there naked, I saw her eyes linger.

"Maybe *I* should take a photo," she said, pulling on the robe. "I should paint you. I could use *you* for one of *my* studies."

I walked over to the dresser and found a pair of boxers. "I'll let you when you let me paint you nude." I could always do it from memory, but I would definitely have to get her consent to do that.

"Ah, never mind," she said, tying the robe. She gave me a bashful look as if she wasn't about to make that trade. "I'll just go down and take that shower now." As she headed to the stairs, I followed.

Once in the living room, I walked over to where I had undressed her and helped her pick up her clothes. "There's a brand-new toothbrush in the cabinet if you want it."

"Thanks. I'll take you up on that." She took her clothes to the bathroom, and a minute later, while I made coffee, she turned on the shower.

I had just taken the first sip of my coffee when Puck walked into the apartment, looking around. "Is she still here?"

"Yeah, she's in the bathroom getting a shower. She has to get to her house to change for work, so I'll need you to take me to the gallery where I left my car."

"No problem. Do you mind if I grab a cup of coffee too? I ran out of K-Cups downstairs. I need to go to the store."

"It's cool. I'm sure she'd love to say hello."

Puck grabbed his cup and made himself a cup of coffee, then went to the kitchen table and took out his phone. "Come look at this, Chris. You've got to give me your honest opinion on this now. I was talking with Jules, and she likes dogwoods and mockingbirds. I thought about adding a few wild berries to the mix as well. She wants something natural-looking, and that reminded her of visiting her grandmother's house."

"It's gorgeous." I couldn't believe the detail that would have to go into it. "You're really branching out. I think this is going to be your best piece ever."

"Do you think I could pull it off?" he asked, giving me a look like he wanted me to be a hundred percent honest with him.

"I think you've got it," I said. "I've seen a lot of improvement, and if anyone can pull that off in ink, it's you."

"Thanks. You really inspired me by stepping out of your comfort zone a little with your last project, and well, I guess from the sound of that shower, it's a good sign that things are working out for you." He waggled his brows.

"You'll do well, my friend. This is your year. You got this." Puck had come a long way with his art, and he had balls I didn't have to put his art on living canvases. I respected the hell out of him for that. It wasn't something any artist could do.

The shower shut off, and then a few minutes later, Hope walked out. "Good morning, Puck," she said, and then she turned to me. "Are you sure I don't need to drop you off?"

"It's cool. Don't be late on my account. Come on; I'll walk you out."

I glanced back at Puck, whose face had a big smirk. "Bye, Hope," he said. "See you later."

She said goodbye, and then we went down through the shop and to the back door where she was parked. "Call me later?"

I tried my best to look like I thought it was a chore. "Okay, I guess so." I huffed but then gave her a big smile. "You know I will."

"Okay," she said, trying to play nonchalant. "I mean, if you do, you do."

I put my arms around her and pulled her closer. "I will."

She went up on her toes, and we shared a nice, long kiss before she had to pull away. "I've got to go."

"If you must," I said. She drove away, and I went back into the house to find Puck eating a bowl of cereal at the table.

"She's pretty fucking amazing, my friend."

"Isn't she, though?" I went back to my coffee and then poured another cup.

"Oh, sure. Have you read the reviews? You're both hits." He pushed his phone across the table when I sat down with him. He had brought up an article from the local press.

The headline read: *Artist and his Muse Imitate Life.* I read the review and found it to be a positive one. Most others were as well, and it appeared that the two of us had gotten off to a really great start.

CHAPTER 8

HOPE

After a few calls and texts through the weekend, which I thought would be enough, I was itching to see Chris in person again.

I had hoped that he'd show up at Paddy's for more supplies, but then he'd told me that he had been busy with his mother and Puck, so I didn't want to seem too eager.

I really liked him, but I knew it was still so early in our relationship, if that's what I should call it. It wasn't that I had doubts that he liked me, and it was undeniable that he had some kind of infatuation with the way he had painted me, but what if had already gotten me out of his system?

I tried to push those thoughts from my mind on Monday morning as I walked into art class.

"Good morning, Hope," Professor Simon greeted me. "How does it feel to be recognized in a truly striking piece of art?"

"It was a little intense, actually. It's not like I had any prior knowledge Chris had used me as a model."

"That's what he said, but I was referring to the reviews about you."

"Reviews?" I hadn't expected any reviews. I wasn't the artist, and it wasn't like anyone really knew me aside from my classmates and Chris.

"Yes. Surely you've seen them?" He gave me a look as if I should know all about it.

"Do you mean Chris's? For his painting? I'm afraid I haven't seen any reviews. Where could I read them?"

"Just google Christian Tate, and I'm sure you'll find something." He went back to his desk and sat down as the others arrived for class.

I went to my desk and took out my phone to use the time before class to look for the reviews. Why hadn't Chris mentioned anything? It seemed strange that he hadn't. Maybe they were bad?

Just as an article pulled up, showing Chris standing in front of the painting of me, Rosa walked into class.

"There's the lady of the hour." She took her station next to me. It was then I noticed a few of the other girls giving me dirty looks.

Rosa noticed too. "Hey," she said. "Don't let them get to you. And about those reviews, just remember that everyone has opinions. It doesn't mean they're right."

"Why do you say that? Did someone say something bad about me? I just heard there were reviews."

"No, actually, for the most part, you and Christian did well. But there was an exposé; it talked about your relationship."

"Our relationship? We don't really—"

She didn't wait for me to finish. "Say what you want, but I'd check out the reviews and the photos before you deny anything."

My heart began to pound. What on earth did she mean? I hurried to read the articles the search engine pulled up, including one that said Chris and I were a couple. The article showed the two of us walking hand in hand at the Grind and then entering the tattoo parlor. There was a blurb that pondered if we had gotten matching tattoos to mark our big night. And another one that speculated we'd been secretly dating for months and were just waiting on the show to make our debut. While some of the articles seemed positive, even though most of their information was wrong, some had ugly things to say about the idea of an artist dating his muse, and how it was an antiquated publicity stunt, and shame on us both.

I left class feeling sick, and by the time I bumped into Nicole, she was concerned by my appearance. "Are you okay?"

"Yeah, it's just that there were some things printed about the other night. I guess I wasn't ready for that kind of feedback, and then there's a lot of rumors and speculation. I don't want it to turn Chris off of me."

A few of the girls from class passed by, giving me dirty looks.

"What's their problem?" Nicole asked. "Whose ass do I need to kick?" She glared at the girls and gave them the evil eye.

"I'm not sure. They must have read the articles. There were some saying I was just a publicity stunt. Do you think that could be true?" It made me sick to think about it.

"No, and as for those girls, they're just jealous that you're getting the attention. They need to remember this is college and not high school, but then, you know how petty some bitches can be."

"I don't care about them. I only care about what Chris thinks."

"Well, don't let it get you down. I've got to run, but I'll call you later and we'll figure this out."

I gave her a quick hug, and then we parted ways. And by the time I made it to my car, I had another problem. My father.

When he called, I stared at the photo on my phone. I didn't want to answer it. What if he had seen the reviews? He was already giving me hell about moving to Chicago and going to school. And the fact that I'd taken summer classes instead of going home to spend the summer with him hadn't gone over well either. Especially since he despised art. What would he think if he found out about Chris and me?

The call went to voicemail, and I breathed a sigh of relief and started the car. But then the phone rang again, and it was him. Again. Mr. Persistent. I should have known he was going to keep calling.

"Hey, Daddy," I said, waiting for him to bring up Chris or the painting of me.

"Hey, Dumplin', I'll be in town for a few days. I wanted to see you later tonight."

Just hearing that he was in town was enough to make my stomach hurt. "I can't tonight. I have to work."

He groaned. "Can't you take the night off? You and I both know that job isn't your future. And I haven't seen you in months."

"No, Daddy. I can't just call in because you want to hang out. Besides, I have to close. I promised Jude I'd fill in for my coworker tonight." I felt a little relief that he hadn't brought up the painting or Chris.

"Fine then, what about tomorrow? You don't have

school on Tuesday, right?" His voice was firm, and I could tell he was already feeling slighted from the tone.

I knew I had better not argue with him. "I am off tomorrow," I said, knowing that my plans to relax and hopefully see Chris had just been shot to hell.

"Perfect. I'll see you then. We'll have lunch. We have business to discuss, you and me."

"Business?" My heart sank. He was going to try and push me into the family business, I just knew it. And when I refused, things would get ugly. Just like always. "Sounds good."

"I'll text you the information to my room, and you can meet me there at 9:00 a.m. I'd like to see you bright and early. We'll make the most of the day."

"Yes, sir."

"I love you, Dumplin'." Even with the endearment, his tone was hard.

"I love you too, Dad. I'll see you soon." I got a rumble in my gut from him springing a visit. It wasn't ever a good thing.

Even after we hung up, the anticipation of having to see him, of knowing that it was just going to be more arguing and him trying to control my life, made my stomach feel like I'd swallowed a soldering iron.

I hurried up and made it to work, trying hard not to call in and curl up in my bed for the remainder of my day.

Work went by slowly, and it was almost closing time when I finally heard from Chris. And this time, he didn't call or text.

"I thought I'd come down and see if you're earning your keep around here."

"Ah, so you're really a spy for Paddy's. That makes sense. The whole artist thing, it was a front, wasn't it?"

"You caught me. Couldn't you tell from that horrible piece of art?" I found his playful attitude refreshing.

"Hey, now, that horrible piece of art has gotten us some attention. Although, I'm not quite sure it's the kind I wanted." I hated to worry him about it, but I was still terrified my father was going to find out about us and the painting.

He studied my expression a moment, then leaned on the counter and took my hand. "What's got you down? The reviews looked good from what I saw the other day."

"There was an exposé in today's paper, Chris. It made a few assumptions, posted a photo of us going to the tattoo parlor and walking down your street holding hands."

"Ah, I see. Well, it's not a secret we're spending time together, is it?" He stroked my hand with his thumb. "You don't have another man in your life that you didn't tell me about, do you?"

"No, well, not really."

He pulled his hand away. "What's going on, Hope?" I could tell he didn't like that from his frown.

"It's my *father*. He doesn't know about us, and I don't want him to be angry at me for not mentioning it."

"Didn't you tell me he lives outside the city? He probably won't find out."

"He lives in New York. Except for this week, he's in Chicago, and he wants to see me tomorrow." I knew it was impossible to hide my emotions when it came to talking about my father.

"Is it that bad?"

I didn't want to tell him about New York and how my father had been trying to get me to move back home and work with him and the family business since I'd first moved to Chicago. "We don't get along. And it always ends in a fight. He's threatened to disown me, and look, I don't want to get into it." I held on to my stomach, which was tying in knots.

He patted my hand. "It's cool. You don't have to explain. My mother is complicated too, at times."

"Does she try to control you?" I didn't think anyone could be as bad as my father.

"In the past, she was a lot worse about it, but yeah, I think parents believe if they made you, they should get to control you for the rest of their lives. But now, I just keep her at arm's length when I can and try not to let her get me down."

"I wish it were that easy. And I guess my day off tomorrow is screwed too. I had hoped I could see you."

"Well, when do you get out of here?"

I looked at the clock. It was time for the store to be closing. There weren't any customers and hadn't been for at least an hour before he had arrived. Jude was working in the back, and she would lock up.

"Actually, I am free to go once I close my register. Did you want to make a purchase?"

"No. I just came to see you. You're all I need from Paddy's tonight."

I felt my body tingle, and I was so glad he wanted to hang out. "I'll just be a minute."

"I'd say take your time, but really, I kind of hope you hurry up." He made a circular gesture with his hands as if to tell me to hurry along, but his sly smile let me know he was only teasing.

"Can't wait to get me alone, huh?" I wondered what kind of kinky things he'd want to do with me.

"Yeah, I've got big plans for us."

"Big plans?"

"Huge." He opened his arms wide.

I didn't ask any questions. Instead, I opened my cash register as he walked to the bench by the door to wait for me. Then, when I had the register empty, I walked to the back to find Jude and gave her the money.

When I walked out front, I smiled inside as Chris got to his feet and held out his hand. For once, it was nice to have someone waiting for me after work. *I could get used to this.*

CHAPTER 9

CHRIS

"Are you sure about this?" he asked. "If you don't want to do it, then just say something now. Things are about to get really messy up in here. And once we get started, there's no turning back." I needed her to know exactly what she was getting into.

"I trust you. But I'm not sure about the naked part."

I needed her completely comfortable for what I had in mind. "Do you have a bikini?" I asked.

"Not on me," she said, giving me a look like I was crazy. "I do have on an adorable bra and panties set. Could you paint them to look like a bikini?"

I pretended like I needed to think about it. "Hm. I don't know. I'd have to see them. I guess you're going to have to take off your clothes." I tried my hardest not to smirk.

She looked into my eyes. "Keep your eyes here on mine until I say otherwise." She pointed two fingers in my direction, then pointed back to her eyes. "Right here."

I did as she commanded. "You do remember that I've seen you naked before, right?"

She smiled big. "I know, but I'm going to see how long you can last without peeking." She took off her shirt and then unzipped her jeans as we stared into each other's eyes.

But then, when I heard the zipper, I couldn't help it. I had to see what she was unwrapping.

"You are horrible." She gave me a little push. "You can't keep your eyes off of me."

"Well, you do make it hard."

"Fair enough." She stripped off her jeans and then tossed them over to where her shoes lay next to the bed.

Her dark purple bra and panties were the perfect color to complement the rest of the painting. "I think I can work with that." I felt my body respond as she walked over to the clean, white drop cloth.

She looked down at it and touched it with her toe as if testing the waters. "Now, explain this to me again, please."

"You're going to lie down on the drop cloth. I'll pose you, and then I'm going to paint your skin. When I have the look I want, I'll snap a few photos and then—"

"Ravish my body?" She batted her lashes and looked up at me, her chin resting on her shoulder as if she were playing innocent.

She made me hard when she talked that way. "If you keep up that talk, yes."

She lay back on the cloth, and I walked over to the paint and got started preparing the colors. I chose things that would play off her hair, and when I had them selected, I walked over with the first paint and knelt down beside her.

As I dragged the soft brush across her tummy, she giggled. "You have to be still, Hope." I smiled, looking down at how playful she looked, curled up and giggling. Inspiration struck me again as I painted a blue swirl on her hip.

She drew up her legs and giggled louder when I went for the other color.

"What is wrong with you?" I asked with a giggle. Her laughter was contagious.

"I can't help it. It tickles."

I came back with a bright green and then knelt down to do a wide stripe down one side of her arm. "I'll try not to make it tickle," I said, knowing once I got close to her armpit, she was going to lose control.

And I wasn't wrong.

By the time I had that done, she had tears in her eyes. "I'm sorry."

"Okay, so when I say freeze, I want you to hold your pose. Whatever pose you're in, do you got it?"

I had a series of intricate shapes and swirls painted across her body, and some that bled down to the canvas. But instead of fighting against her sensitivity, I decided to use it. I readied my camera and then dragged a dry brush down her ticklish spot along her side.

She reacted, pulling away, her smile spreading ear to ear as she laughed. "Freeze!" I said, snapping the photo. The result was much better than I'd thought it would be, and I was surprised when I didn't even need another photo. But I took a few quick ones anyway.

"Did you get it?" she asked, still laughing. "Please tell me you did. This is torture."

"I did. Come look."

"You mean I can get up?"

"Yes, I'm done." I was so ready to start the painting that I let the excitement take hold. "Look at how amazing that is. You look like you're so happy."

"You make me that way," she said. "Even I can't believe how good that looks. And I never really like photos of myself. You capture something in me. Something I don't usually realize is there."

"You're a natural." I didn't see how she wasn't a model. She had a gift. Part of me was glad I'd discovered her first because I was going to show her off to the world. "Now, I just have to paint you.

"How many canvases are you going to use?"

"For this? Just one. And if you're up to it, I'd like to make an entire series of you."

"Really? Won't that get boring?"

She had to be kidding. "Bored of you? Of this? I don't think so."

Hope looked at the photo again. "It's hard to believe I'm so worried about seeing my father tomorrow. I guess I'm a better actress than I thought."

"Don't let it get to you. The night is ours. Not his. He can't have you until tomorrow." I didn't like sharing her with anyone, even him.

Hope seemed to like that. She looked down at the paint that was covering her body. "Now that you've made a mess out of me, I think it's time that you clean me up." She stepped closer, reaching up to put her arms around my neck even though she had to get on her tiptoes to do it.

I bent down to accommodate her, and as we kissed, I reached around and stripped off the bra. "I should get you undressed if I'm going to clean you up." I let my breath hit her ear and smiled as her's hitched.

Keeping the lip lock, I lifted her up against me and carried her downstairs to the bathroom. The front door was locked, and since Puck had seen us come up together, he knew the drill. His ass was going to sleep on the downstairs couch again.

I put her back on her feet and then turned on the water

to get the right temperature. Then I turned and looked down at her painted body, thinking of how I was going to pay careful attention to every single inch of it.

I knelt down and hooked my fingers into her panties, then slipped them down as she watched.

Hope reached for my hand and then stepped into the shower, under the spray. "You have work to do," she said.

"Don't worry; I'll be thorough." I stepped in with her and then took the bath gel and lathered it in my hands. I reached for her soft mound, where the little tuft of hair was a perfect landing strip. Everything about her made me hard, right down to the way the suds ran down her body, over the peaks and valleys. It mixed with the paint, creating a rainbow that pooled at our feet before washing down the drain.

Once I had her supple skin polished to a fine shine, I knelt down and caressed her bottom as I kissed her mound, parting her folds with my tongue, which I dragged up her slit to play with her clit. When I slipped two fingers inside of her, I didn't relent.

She moaned as I brushed that tender spot, and then she rolled her head back in ecstasy as I worked her to her first orgasm.

After she regained her composure, she encouraged me to my feet and took my cock into her hands. She stroked my erection, her fingers dancing across the veiny flesh, her thumb rolling across the head. "I want you inside me, Chris." She looked up into my eyes, and I wasn't about to make her ask me twice. Especially when she turned and faced the shower wall and glanced back at me over her shoulder.

I moved behind her but knew better than to make any assumptions about how adventurous she was willing to get.

I stroked her pussy with my cock, dragging the head through her folds, parting them to nudge against her sopping wet channel. She was more than ready for me, and I could barely hold out any longer.

I pushed into her, and she tensed at first but then relaxed, my cock gliding into her and burying deep. I rutted forward, my hips bouncing off the soft curves of her ass as our bodies slapped together as if applauding us for our efforts.

I reached around her front and rolled her clit between my fingers as I thrust inside of her, and as if we were well-tuned and timed machines, we found our releases at the same time.

"That was amazing," she said, collapsing against the wall. "But I don't want you to stop."

"Oh, don't worry, baby. We're only getting started." I was already primed and ready for round two. "Let's go the bed."

She giggled and turned to kiss me. I took her hand and led her to the bed, where I gave her everything I had promised.

We made love well into the morning, and, after a few hours' sleep, it was heaven waking up with her warm little body pressed against mine.

I stroked her face and kissed her cheek. She opened her eyes and then snuggled closer. "Good morning," she whispered.

"Good morning," I replied. "Do you want me to make breakfast, or do you want to go to the Grind?"

"Shit!" She bolted upright. "What time is it?"

"Eight. Why?" She hadn't said anything about being awake at a specific time, and there were still a few hours to go before having lunch with her father.

She got out of the bed, grabbed my robe, and then ran downstairs. I got up and followed, curious about why she was acting like her ass was on fire.

"Hey, are you just going to wham, bam, thank you, man me?"

Hope picked up her phone and held her stomach. "Oh shit. He tried to call me. I left my phone down here."

"So, call him back."

"Chris, I've got to be at my father's hotel at nine. He's going to be so upset if I'm late."

"I'm sure he'll understand. Tell him there was traffic." She was freaking out for nothing.

"You don't get it. He doesn't understand shit. And I have to go home and change my underwear, which has paint all over it." She went back upstairs, and I followed. "I can't go looking like this."

She held her stomach. "I'm going to throw up."

"Are you sick?"

"No, he always makes me feel this way. I swear, I probably have an ulcer from dealing with him. I'm constantly ill just hearing his voice."

"You shouldn't let him get to you. Get dressed, and I'll drive you home. I'll Uber back. You don't need to be driving as upset as you are, especially in a hurry."

"I'm good, I promise. I should go." She hurried and dressed, and even though I tried to convince her otherwise, she left on her own.

It had been such a good night to end so crappy. I had to admit it didn't win any points for her father.

By the time I had gotten home, changed into something decent to meet my father, left a text to say I was running late, and finally made it across town to his hotel, it was nearly eleven fifteen. I was pulling up when my phone rang. He couldn't even give me time to get there.

"Where are you?" he scolded.

"I had a little trouble in traffic. I got trapped behind someone who had a flat, and they couldn't drive over forty." It sounded like a reasonable excuse to me, but I knew it wouldn't change his mood. "I'm pulling up outside now."

"I see you," he said, sounding as if he was disappointed. "I'm walking out the door."

I looked up to see him stepping out under the awning, and I drove around, avoiding the valet lane, to pick him up.

He opened the door and got into the passenger seat. "I could have arranged a car," he said. "But I figured you should know the city well enough now. I guess I was wrong."

"It's not that. It was the person with the flat." I didn't want to fight.

"Where were you last night?" he asked.

I thought for a moment he had learned about Chris and me, and my heart nearly stopped. "What do you mean? I had to work."

He gave me a pointed look as he fastened his seat belt. "I called you after ten. You didn't answer."

I had forgotten about the missed calls. "My phone was dead."

"That's why you need the landline. If you had one, I wouldn't have to rely on your cell phone to get my calls. You'd be there to answer when I needed you."

"I don't need a landline. No one has those anymore, but you." I only knew of a handful who still paid the regular phone company anything.

"Well, I trust you can choose an appropriate restaurant. Somewhere that has a good steak and not some shriveled-up piece of leather." He had always been a snob about fine dining. Not many could cook a steak, much less anything else to suit him.

I was sure wherever I chose, it wouldn't be good enough for him. He hated Chicago and despised that I lived there.

I drove him to the nicest fine-dining restaurant that I knew of, a cute little place called Blue Spoon.

We waited for nearly half an hour for a table, and when we were seated, my father wasn't happy with where it was located. "Who wants to sit in the middle of the goddamned entrance?" he said to the waitress. "Don't you have something in the back?"

"I'm sorry, sir, if you and your girlfriend want to wait a while longer, I'm sure that—"

"She's my daughter! And no, we won't wait. I see a table empty back there. We'll take that one." He walked past the waitress, and I gave her a sympathetic look as my father proceeded to the table and plopped his ass in the chair. "We'll have your finest wine, please. And I want your best appetizer." He snapped his fingers as I sank into my seat.

"You could please do us both the courtesy of not pissing off the staff. I'd like to have a spit-free dining experience. Besides, she's just doing her job." I didn't know why I expected to have a nice meal with him for once. I couldn't remember the last time I'd eaten with him without a burning coal in my gut.

My father huffed. "Maybe if you hadn't set the mood by making me wait, I'd have a little more patience."

"Can we just move past that and try to have a nice time?"

He looked up from his menu. "I'll have a nice time when the wine gets here," he said.

"It's barely noon," I said.

"And your point is?" He took the bottle from the waiter who brought it. "Thank you, I can pour it myself."

He poured us each a glass as the waiter walked away, shaking his head.

After we ordered, a few minutes later, my father finally had enough wine in him to want to talk to me. "So, I was thinking that we should talk about your salary. I'm prepared to offer you a considerable bonus for taking the position, and since your aunt Mary left, you'd have the top-floor office next to mine."

"I'm not interested in Aunt Mary's office or more money. I've already told you that I like it here."

He took out his phone. "Well, I had hoped that if I

entertained you here a while, you'd realize how little this place has to offer and come to your senses. But since you hadn't come home, yet I thought I'd better see just what you were up to."

"You've hardly entertained anything. You've bullied me the entire way, and I'm not up to anything that you don't know all about."

"Well, I'd have to disagree," he said, sliding his phone across the table. "Go ahead. Take a look."

I glanced down to see the photo of and me, the one walking into the tattoo parlor. "Where did you get that?" I knew damned well; I just needed to know what he had heard.

"Your aunt Mary called me. She was afraid you'd gone and committed another atrocity with your body. But I told her that my daughter, despite the pink dye seeping into her brain, would never get a tattoo. Please tell me I was right at least about that much."

I glanced around, hoping no one was listening and thankful my dad had bullied us into the back, so not as many could witness my scolding. "I didn't get a tattoo. And Chris is a friend."

He looked utterly disgusted. "Chris, is it? I guess that explains why you couldn't answer the phone last night, and why you weren't at your apartment."

I realized I was busted. Of course he'd come by my apartment to snoop on me. "Is this why you came to Chicago?"

"No, but it's why *you* have to *leave* it. You're not throwing your life away to be some tortured artist's muse. I need you back home, and you have a duty to your family to take your place in the family business. I don't see why it's so hard for you to understand."

"And I don't see why it's so hard for you to see why I don't want it. Look at Aunt Mary. She's just retired, and she's all alone. She's given everything she has to the business, and I'm not going to do that. I want to do something that makes me happy."

"Like what? There's nothing for you here. And since you want to play hardball, I'm not giving you any choice. I'm going to cancel the lease on the apartment at the end of the month, and as for your allowance, I'm cutting that off as well. You'll have your trust, but I'm sure you'll find out really fast how hard it is to be on your own. You can keep the car, of course, you know, in case you need a place to live."

He really thought I wouldn't make it? I was determined to prove him wrong. "I'm not coming home."

"Why? You have nothing here. And that man you've been entertaining, he's going to get bored like all artists do, and then you'll be left all alone, with nothing. I can cut you off, you know—and I don't just mean the allowance. I mean from any inheritance you're going to see. All it would take is a phone call."

I couldn't believe he was threatening me. I had a trust worth five hundred fifty thousand that I was just sitting on until the day I could dip into it. Although it didn't mature until I was twenty-nine, I could pay my rent on the trust allowance, and maybe, if I scrimped and saved, I could manage on my salary at Paddy's. I'd rather make it work than go home to someone who was holding money over me in exchange for my happiness.

"If that's what you want to do to me, I can't stop you. I can only try to be happy despite your cruelty."

"You think I'm being mean?" he mocked me and then took another sip of wine.

"You're bullying me, just like you used to do to Mom." I knew that wasn't going to sit well with him, but it was the truth. He had bullied her into an early grave.

"Your mother did that to herself."

"Right, because she was the only one of you with a drug or alcohol problem, right?" My mother had a problem with prescription medicine that had gotten out of control. She overdosed when I was in high school, and it had been the old man and me ever since.

"Well, I'm not going to be her. I'm not going to try and fit into your world just to wither away because I can't. I want to finish college, get my degree, and start my own company."

"Doing what? You don't know anything. Or anyone. Our connections are back home, and if you think I'm going to give you a leg up for anything else, you're crazy. You need to stop being a spoiled brat and know your place."

He pounded his fist on the table, and the wineglasses rattled along with the silverware.

I took a few deep breaths and was thankful when our food was brought out. Even though my stomach was sick, I ate anyway, hoping that it would keep my mouth busy. I had way too much I wanted to say, but he wasn't going to want to hear any of it.

As he ate his steak, carving into the meat, he looked up from his plate. "So, who is this Chris person? I saw the painting he did of you. I guess he's some kind of artist? Is this what you're doing now? Modeling?"

"I didn't model for him. He surprised me with it at his gallery opening."

"So, you didn't even get paid? What kind of business-woman are you? *If* that painting sells, he's going to end up with a nice chunk of change. You should make sure you get some of that." He shoved the steak in his mouth. "You never know when you'll need the money."

"I'm not interested in his money."

"Which means that he must not have any."

"Wrong. He's a successful artist, and he owns the building in the photo."

My father laughed. "Successful artist. Look, I'd make sure he understands that your stay here is not a permanent one. I'm giving you until the end of the month. You need to square away your school, get yourself transferred back home, and you can finish that degree of yours at night if you're so hell-bent on having it. If you're not going to cooperate, at least heed my warning. Things are about to get a hell of a lot harder for you."

He didn't even show any emotion with his words. "Why does it make you happy to see me so miserable?"

"You don't know misery, Hope. Misery is not being able to eat. Misery is sleeping in your car. Go ahead, go ask a homeless man."

"I have my trust, and you can't touch it."

"That trust is going to give you a few crumbs at best before you can fully access it. And by the time you get it, you'll be so far in debt it won't do you a lick of good. We'll see how long you can manage."

He went quiet again, carving his steak and gorging himself on it. He didn't bother speaking to me again, and when he was done, he got up from the table and called himself a cab, leaving me with the check that included his four-hundred-dollar bottle of wine.

It wasn't any wonder he made me sick. I took the remainder of the bottle and poured a glass. I contemplated going back home, letting him win, but the harder he bullied me, the more I wanted to fight back. It wasn't just a matter of being happy and the fact that Chris was in my life, because I wasn't really sure where that was going, but staying was about showing my father who was really the boss when it came to my life.

CHAPTER 11

CHRIS

After giving Hope the time that she needed with her father, I decided to surprise her on Wednesday by showing up at the end of Professor Simon's art class.

I knocked softly on the door and stuck my head inside, puzzled when she wasn't amongst the others in the class.

"Well, this is certainly a treat," Professor Simon said.

I glanced over to the sinks to see if she was up cleaning out her brushes or if perhaps she had needed some napkins. When I didn't see her, I realized I must look like an idiot for popping in, so I thought of something quickly. "I wanted to stop in and see how your students liked the show and see if you wanted to set something up soon regarding getting their art in the gallery."

I had already talked to Virginia about doing a student exhibit in the lobby. Something that would include the community as we welcomed them.

"Oh, well, feel free to look around. I'm sure you'll be inspired by some of my other students as well. I'm afraid your Ms. Mayhew is not here today."

"Is she ill?" I asked.

Professor Simon gave me a look. "I'd think you'd know more about her than me. All I know is she didn't show."

"I see. Well, let me have a look around while you look at your calendar. You might want to give the students some time to get something together."

"Of course, thank you. Make yourself at home."

The other students all welcomed me, and I killed some time walking around the room. When I came to an empty station in the back, I stopped and took another look.

"That's where Hope sits," the girl closest to her station said. "She's pretty good."

I looked at the painting that was propped up on the canvas. "She did this one?" It was colorful and vibrant in a way I had always hoped to achieve, and it inspired me just as she had.

"Yes. Professor Simon lets us leave them here from Monday, so we don't have to bring them back and forth. She was supposed to finish today."

"I see." I had remembered him doing that when I was there, but I couldn't focus on anything but the painting in front of me. The landscape was magical, with a large tree depicted in the middle and on each side, the different seasons. It was a painting concept I'd seen many times, and while the composition wasn't anything new, the color scheme and atten-tion to detail was amazing. She used heavy brush strokes, and the texture it gave the piece set a mood. It was beautiful.

"She's got a way with color, doesn't she?" I asked the girl. Who knew my muse was a true artist herself? It was just like how she had chosen the pink hair that made her look like a walking piece of art. The painting matched her style.

"She is. I think the only problem she has is with her confidence."

I had a pretty good idea who was killing creative that spirit. Her father. And seeing how she hadn't come to school, it made me worry if things were much worse than she had let on.

I finished up at the college, leaving Professor Simon's class with a new appreciation for Hope. She was not only beautiful, funny, smart, and downright amazing, she was talented on top of it.

But I couldn't help but worry that something was terribly wrong. Had she gotten in an accident? Had she fallen ill?

I drove to the apartment building she'd told me about, which was a little fancier than I'd imagined, with enough security that at least I wouldn't have to worry about her safety. The security guard took my name, and then she gave me permission to go up.

"Thank you," I said, as the guard opened the door.

"She's in 2B."

I went to the elevator, and when I got out on her floor, she was standing in her doorway down the hall, waving at me.

"Are you okay?" I asked, seeing that she was in her yoga pants and a long shirt with her hair looking a bit limper than usual. It curled up around her ears, and while it wasn't long enough to be too messy, it was still not as tamed as usual and somehow made her look a lot younger.

"I'm fine," she said, stepping out of the way to let me in. "I'm sorry I didn't call. I've been sleeping a lot and doing a lot of thinking."

"I thought you were sick or something. I went to your

class to surprise you earlier and panicked when you weren't there."

She smiled and led me to the living room. "You're sweet, and I didn't mean to make you worry. But I've had a lot on my mind." She sat on the couch where she had a hot cup of coffee and a blanket. "Would you like some coffee?"

"No, thanks." I took the spot next to her. "I'm just glad you're okay. I'm sorry for popping in on you. I can give you space if you need it. I just needed to know that you were okay."

She reached out and took my arm. "It's nice that you care. I sometimes feel a bit lonely in the world since my mother died. My father is as comforting as a stone wall." She took her hand away and then picked up her mug to take a drink.

"Did something happen?"

She gave a soft laugh, but I could tell it was in contradiction to her true feelings. "Just my father. He happened. He always happens."

I angled toward her. "Did he hurt you?" I wasn't sure what kind of relationship they had, or if the man was abusive.

She took a deep breath, then let it out as if the action might cleanse her in some way. "Just my pride. And maybe my self-confidence."

Just hearing her say it, with that soft and fragile voice, made me angry. How could he make her feel that way? "That sucks. What does he have to be such a jerk about?"

She eased back and put her feet up on the table, still holding her cup as if it comforted her. "He's trying to get me to go home to New York City."

"Why? You're doing well here. Why can't he just be happy?"

"I guess because he's not. He's miserable, but then, he's always been that way. I don't know what it's about. Maybe something happened to him as a child. Now that my mother isn't around to take it, I get to."

"Well, that doesn't sound fair. And frankly, it pisses me off. You look like you've been through hell. I can see the emotion in your eyes. You're nearly in tears just talking about him. And he's your father? This isn't normal. Are you sure there isn't more?"

She hesitated a moment, and just when I was about to press, she responded. "He cut me off, and he's threatening to disinherit me."

"You mean when he dies?"

She nodded. "It's all because I won't take my place in the family business. The thing is, I don't want to work for or with him. But I can't tell him that."

"Why not?"

"He won't hear it, for one. And for two, I've tried in subtle ways, but he just doesn't get it. I want to lead my own life. I've seen the way his family is. The way they all treat each other. The way they always treated my mother. No, thanks."

"Well, I think you need to make him understand. He can't force you to live your life how he wants it." I didn't want to lose her to New York. The thought of her having to move made me sick to my stomach.

"Well, it's worse now. My aunt Mary is retired, and I'm supposed to take her place. He's already told me he's cutting off my allowance. And he thinks there's no way I can make it on my own."

"So, you had an allowance. That's how you afford this place. I had a feeling it wasn't your Paddy's paycheck."

"I found out about Paddy's in the job listings. I thought

it would be easy, and maybe give me a little bit more of an introduction to art since I was taking my first real class. Besides, it gave me extra money to do whatever I wanted and a sense of being on my own. At least an idea."

"Speaking of your art class. I saw your painting. The tree. It's gorgeous." I hated to change the subject, but I could tell she needed a little boost in her confidence. Maybe I could start to repair the damage her father had done.

She gave me a look as if she didn't agree. "You're just being sweet."

"No, I'm serious. Do you have any idea how many artists would kill for your eye for color? It's amazing. I've been trying to develop that for years. It's natural for you. That's a gift."

"Well, I didn't get it from my father. He thinks art is a waste of time."

"So, he's going to cut you off and leave you penniless? So, what happens?"

"I lose my allowance and have to live on what little of my trust I get before I'm thirty. I'll still have to work at Paddy's to eat, and I'll probably do better in a much cheaper apartment if I can find one, but I'll make it."

"How can he do that? Even my mother gave me a leg up. It's what parents should do. Especially a father."

"Well, he's not like other fathers. I've had to learn to live with it."

"I'm sorry. I wish it was better for you."

"Having you here is making it better." She held her stomach. "I feel a lot better now. I swear he is going to give me an ulcer."

"Let's not think about him. You can't let him win by getting you down, and no more missing art class."

"I'm going to go to New York for the weekend. I think if I go home for a few days, it might pacify him."

"I think you're just giving him what he wants." I didn't want her to go. I wanted the weekend to spend with her.

"Well, I need to at least try. This is my life we're talking about. I need to convince him that once I get through this next year and get my business degree, then I'll go back."

"Are you?"

"Am I what?"

"Going to go back to New York once you have your degree?" I felt like she was already getting further away from me. And I hated that she would ever cave to her father's plans.

"Eventually, who knows, but I'm only buying time, Chris. He's been like this before. Besides, now he knows about us. He saw the reviews and the photo of us. He's going to make it a lot more difficult. If I go home, he'll think it wasn't anything serious, and then he'll calm down."

"So, this was about me?"

She let out a long breath. "No, this isn't about you. It's about my father and his need to control everyone around him. Especially me."

"But if I hadn't put you on display, you wouldn't be going through all of this. I'm really sorry."

"It's fine," she said, shifting uncomfortably in her seat. "I'm just glad we met."

"I could have just gone back to Paddy's and asked you out like a normal person. I could have prepared you for the critics. Something." I felt like a complete ass for not doing more to take care of her.

"You don't have anything to apologize for." She got up and went to the kitchen with her coffee cup. On the way, she stopped and looked a bit dizzy.

"Are you all right?"

"I'm just tired. I think I need to go and lie down."

"I could stay if you want. I was supposed to meet with Puck, but I could call and cancel."

"No, it's okay. I just need a little rest. I didn't sleep too well last night." She yawned, and I realized I needed to give her a little space.

I got up and walked over to her. I put my hands on her waist and kissed her lips softly. "I'll call you later."

She smiled at me. "Okay, I'll keep my phone on."

As I left her apartment wondering if she was going to give in to her father or not, she texted me the answer before I got to the car.

I'm just going for the weekend. But I'll keep in touch the whole time I'm there.

"Dammit." There wasn't anything I could do to make her change her mind.

CHAPTER 12

HOPE

As my plane landed back in Chicago on Sunday, I felt a little better about things with my father and couldn't wait to see Chris. As I walked into the airport, fresh off of the plane, Nicole was there waiting for me.

She had been the one to drop me off, and I was excited to see my friend and tell her all about the trip, and more importantly, how Chris and I were getting along.

Nicole ran up to me and gave me a hug. "How was it? Is the Big Apple still rotten?"

"The old man sure is," I said. "But not as much of a crab apple as he was when I first arrived. I think I've managed to convince him that Chris and I are not that serious. Which was hard to do with us texting each other every five minutes."

"Sounds like you two are off to a good start," she said, walking with me to baggage claim.

"So far, so good. But I think he's still a little miffed at me for giving in to my father even for the weekend. I think he's just spoiled for wanting to spend the time with me. At least I hope."

"Well, at least he spent the time texting you. You don't have to question where he was or who he was doing."

"Oh, wow, thanks for that visual." I didn't realize how much something like that would bother me until she said it. "I hadn't really thought of it that way."

"You really like him, don't you?" Nicole asked on the way to the parking lot.

"Yeah, I really do. I mean, you know we were together that couple of times, and I don't usually move that fast, but it's different with him."

"I think it is too. At least, *you're* different. You're not worried about him or if he likes you the way you normally worry over a guy."

"He really puts me at ease. I was so upset I couldn't sleep the other day, and then he came over, and I actually was able to sleep."

"I'm not sure a man who puts you to sleep is something to brag about." She belted a laugh.

"It's hard to explain. I mean, I still have worries. Hoping it's not going to end is a big one, and that he's into me as much as I'm into him, but when we're together, we're so easygoing, if that makes any sense. It's comfortable."

"It's too early to be that comfortable. You don't think it's because you slept together a bit too soon?" She gave me a worried look.

I couldn't believe her. "You're the one who told me to go for it."

She held up her hand in defense. "I know, and I don't think you made a mistake, it's just that sex tends to make people feel closer to one another."

I had to admit she had a point. "Maybe. I guess. It's just different with him. He's special."

She chuckled. "I'd be hot for him too if he painted me. I mean, you know he's into you if he spent that amount of time and detail recreating your body. I only hope he pays that close of attention to you under the sheets."

"Who has time for sheets?" I said. "And yes, he does. He's very attentive." I could feel my body heating up just thinking about him. I couldn't help but want to see him.

Which was why, when we arrived back at the house, I texted him to tell him I was home.

But by the time Nicole left, he still hadn't answered. He didn't answer when I called either. Feeling a little disappointed, I wondered if he'd walked downstairs.

Even though I didn't want to be obsessive, I called the tattoo shop.

"This is Puck," his friend answered. "What can I do you for?"

"Hi Puck, it's Hope. I was just wondering if Chris was around? He's not answering his phone, so I thought maybe he walked downstairs to see you."

"Nah, he's up in the studio working like a wild man. Are you back in town?"

"Yes, and I thought I'd come by and see him. If you think it's okay?"

"Please do. He's been holed up in there since you left. I think the only time he comes down is to take a piss or for food and water. I usually toss him a few crumbs now and then, but I'm sure he'd love to see you."

I felt better knowing Puck approved. "Thanks. I'll be there in about twenty. If he tries to leave, don't let him."

"I'll keep him here. You're good. Just come on in. I'm about to start my next session."

We ended the call, and I went to freshen up a bit and changed clothes. I wanted to be fresh when he saw me, and I hoped that he didn't mind me popping in on him like he had done me.

I drove across the city to his neighborhood, where it always seemed a bit livelier than mine. I pulled in and parked behind the tattoo shop, and then I did just as Puck had requested. I went into the shop and caught him leaning over a man who was getting a tattoo on his back. The man was white-knuckling the chair cushion with a death grip, his jaw set tight and fire in his eyes.

"Just let me know if you need another break, man. It's only going to get worse."

I mouthed a hello as he glanced up and then tiptoed past the two of them to get to the stairs. When I went up, I tapped on the door, but Chris never heard. He had probably fallen asleep.

I checked the door to find it open, so I went inside and looked up at the loft, where I expected him to see me from.

But he had no idea I was there. He was too into what he was doing.

He beat his brush against the canvas and then loaded his brush with paint again only to repeat the action. I listened to the noise all the way up the stairs and thought it was no wonder he hadn't heard the phone, which was on the floor with his shoes and shirt, as he stood there in his paint-stained shorts.

"You weren't kidding. You really do beat the hell out of your brushes."

He spun around, and his eyes narrowed before widening. "Hope."

"Surprise," I said, but then I was surprised when he hurried over, revealing the painting in the background. It was me again, this time lying on the backdrop with the bright colors and shapes behind me, the smile on my face one of contagious happiness. "Wow," I said as he hugged me tightly.

"You're back."

I glanced down at his phone. "If you would answer that thing, you'd already know it."

"It must have died. I haven't plugged it in all day, and I was lost in a trance." He picked it up and checked. "Yeah, it's dead." He walked over and plugged it in next to his bed as I walked over and looked at the canvas.

The mad, wild streaks added chaos to the joy that was in my expression. "Are you almost done?"

"It has a while to go. But I'm just so glad to see you." He hugged me again. "So, how'd it go with your dad?"

I held on to him. "It went well. I missed you."

"I missed you too. Although, I found a really therapeutic way to deal with it." He raked his hand through his hair. "Don't go away again," he said before he kissed me.

"I'll try not to," I said.

He shook his head. "Then I'll just have to make sure you want to stay." He kissed me and then walked me back to his bed, and we stopped just next to it.

"You're so beautiful. Even more beautiful than the painting. It was a horrible substitute." He pulled me closer and then crawled up on the bed as I lay back. He rested on his elbows above me. "I thought about you the entire time."

"I can see that," I said with a laugh. "You're not kidding."

"No. And I'm going to show you how much I missed you." He moved down, stopping to rest between my legs where he undid my jeans and then rose up to take them off. Then he reached for my panties, slipping them down to my knees before touching me, parting my folds to insert his finger in my aching channel.

Once there, he pumped his arm, firmly stroking me until I squirmed. The intense feeling had me even wetter in no time, as my first orgasm broke.

"That's my girl," he whispered, his breath hot against the flesh of my thigh. And then, as if to show me how much better it could get, he kissed me there, taunting and teasing me with his tongue.

Just when I thought I would come undone, he moved up and pulled out his cock, centering it at my entrance before he slowly penetrated me.

As the ecstasy consumed me, I never wanted it to end. How could I move back home and give this up?

CHAPTER 13

CHRIS

As I entered her inch by dripping inch, I realized how glad I was to have her back. I hadn't thought she'd stay away forever, but the weekend had been too long.

I thrust hard against her hips, burying deep. In my relentless rhythm, I found her most sensitive spot, which had her writhing beneath me, moaning as she moved her hips in an eager motion.

It was wild and anxious, and the urgency of it, which had us both panting hard to catch our breaths, made it so much more than it had ever been. As if we needed the other to breathe and live.

"Don't stop," she said, her voice vibrating from the movement. "I'm so close." She held on to me, digging her nails into my flesh as she clenched tight on my cock, milking me through each thrust.

I edged myself through her release, but then there was no holding back once she kissed me, pulling me hard against her mouth as if she needed me to live. I had never felt that kind of connection and passion with another human being.

She not only inspired me, but she made me whole in some strange sort of way.

I thrust wildly, spurred on by the sound of our flesh meeting through each plunge. I pulled out of her and buried myself deep one last time, spilling my hot seed into her in wave after molten wave.

We lay there quiet, our bodies both moving as we panted, catching our breaths.

She looked into my eyes. "It's so good to be back. I'm glad I got things squared away with my father, but it wasn't worth the time away from you."

It was amazing that she felt that way about me. I had been trying hard not to analyze what we had and just let it be. Still, as it became harder and harder to remain oblivious to what it was growing, I found myself with the same feelings. This could really be more.

"Did you get things squared away? Is he still going to cut you off?"

"I got a small reprieve. Just for the semester, but he wants me home for the holidays when I'm finished with school. I'm going to stall it again, but for now, I'm just going to live in the moment."

"And us? What did you tell him?"

"It's just best not to let my dad worry about anything. He'll be in our business, and I just don't want it."

"I understand. But there could come a day when he'll know, right? I mean, I won't be your dirty secret forever, will I?"

"Of course. But let's ease into it." Her eyelids were growing heavy, and though I was feeling a bit slighted, as if she were a tad unsure, and maybe we weren't on the magical wave of synchronicity as I had assumed, I let it go for the moment.

I stayed close, stroking her hair until she fell asleep, but when she rolled to her back, her pink nipples peeking out from the covers, I couldn't help but get the itch to be inside of her again.

Knowing how sleepy she was, there was only one thing to do to feed the itch respectfully, and so I got up and headed to the easel. I moved the one painting away and started another, doing a quick sketch of her figure lying in the crumpled sheets. A quiet repose, she looked so pure and innocent. So vulnerable, I had to capture it, if only for the two of us.

I painted through the night, and in the morning, when the sun shone across her breasts like a laser beam illuminating an angel from heaven, she awoke.

I glanced up to see her feeling the bed next to her, and then she rolled over, stretched, and sat up in the bed. "Why are you way over there?" she asked in a sleepy voice.

"Because if I painted in bed, I'd make a mess."

"You're finishing your painting?"

"Not quite. I thought I'd start a new one." I smiled at her, but she looked down and pulled the sheet up over her breasts before getting to her feet.

"What kind of new one?"

"Come and see. It's beautiful." I gave her a sly look, but it didn't take away the worry in her eyes.

She crossed the room and stepped behind me. "Oh no," she said. "Not nude!"

"You're not nude. You're wearing a sheet."

"Those are my nipples!" she said.

"I know. I've seen them." I couldn't believe she was upset and thought she was joking, but then, she walked back to the bed to find her clothes, which she started shrugging on.

"You should have asked," she said. "That's *my* body."

I was a bit taken aback. Surely, she didn't think I was going to hang that in any gallery. "Hey, it's just for our eyes only."

"And Puck's, I'm assuming. Where do you plan to hang it?"

"Above my bed would be nice. Besides, look how beautiful you are."

"And naked. And in your bed. And I don't need my father seeing that. He already thinks you're taking advantage of me."

"Wait, what? Taking advantage how? He doesn't even know me. I'd never do that."

"He's my father; he doesn't need a sane reason. He's not a reasonable man." She waved her hands as if to brush it off. "Just forget I said anything."

I couldn't believe she thought it was that easy to put away my feelings. "You might be able to bottle his criticism up, let it fester and make you sick, but I can't. I don't appreciate it." I put down the brush and wiped my hands. "So, what did he say. How am I taking advantage?"

"You didn't ask permission to use me as your subject for one, and for two, it's not like I'm getting paid."

"So it's about money? You need me to pay you." I was floored.

"He just felt that by you not getting a contract or hiring me, that you are profiting off of my image. You have to understand, my father is a businessman; it's the way he thinks."

"And how do *you* think?" I wondered if she agreed with him, because, so far, it sure seemed that way.

"Well, it was a surprise, but maybe if I had known ahead of time or had been asked—"

"I see."

"No, don't take it that way." I could tell that she was growing upset too. Her eyes turned red, and she hung her head. "Now you see why I didn't want to talk about him. He ruins everything."

"If you don't want me to paint you, then I won't, Hope."

"I love that you paint me." She got up and walked over to hug me. "I'm just not sure I want my tits out for all to see. I wish you had asked me about that one thing."

"I'm sorry. I can paint the sheet a bit higher. Maybe leave some mystery. I just got carried away. You're beautiful to me, Hope. And you make me feel things I haven't in as long as I can remember."

"Don't be sorry. And don't change it. Maybe it will grow on me. But I don't want Puck to see it."

"Easy enough. I'll gouge his eyes out. I'll make him wear a blindfold when he's upstairs. We'll call it a challenge. He's always up for those. Or, I could dare him. He can't refuse a dare."

She gave me a soft giggle. "You're always making me laugh. It makes it hard to be angry with you."

"I don't want you to be angry with me, Hope. And if you ever feel like I've done something in any way to hurt or humiliate you, I'd like you to talk to me. I only want you to be happy. I painted this because I wanted you to see how *I* see you. How beautiful you are when you're sleeping. It's not like you can look in the mirror to see that."

She raised up on her toes and put her arms around my neck, so I met her lips halfway and gave her a big kiss. She sunk into the embrace, letting it linger.

She pulled away, giving me a reluctant look, but then she gave me one more quick peck. "I have to get dressed and go to class. Then I have to work a double shift. All of that time off they gave me, I promised to make up when I returned. And James, my coworker, he's not letting me forget it."

"Come by after?" I wanted to spend another night and another with her.

"You could come by my house. Give Puck a reprieve from the downstairs sofa?"

"I like that even better." I was just glad she still wanted to see me. It had never occurred to me that she would take the painting that way or be embarrassed to show her body. She was perfect. But I guess her modesty was a part of that.

"Will you come by Paddy's?" she asked. "Or just meet me there?"

"Whichever." I pulled her back closer. "Hey, I'll try to do better, okay."

"You're doing amazing. Don't mind me. I just put my foot in my mouth at times, and I guess I was extra hungry this morning."

"No, your feelings shouldn't just be dismissed." I had a feeling her father had been expecting that from her forever. "Could you tell me one thing?"

"Anything," she said.

"I guess I just wanted to know if you're still happy with the way things are going? I feel like we're progressing, aren't we? Or am I crazy?"

"No." She shook her head and let the word hang there until I questioned everything.

"No, I'm not crazy, or this isn't progressing?"

"Oh, you're absolutely crazy, but not about that. I feel it too. I'm happy. Are you happy?"

"Yeah. I guess I was just making sure we're on the same page."

"We are." She gave me one peck. "I'll see you tonight."

She pulled away, and I hesitated to let her go, following her out to the car for one last kiss.

When she left, I watched her drive away and realized that, if I could, I'd spend every waking moment with that woman.

CHAPTER 14

HOPE

Weeks had passed since my return, and Chris and I were getting along so well that it felt like we were a couple. Not only did we talk to each other every single day and have dinner dates at least three times a week, but there wasn't a night that had gone by where I wasn't either at his house or he was at mine. And we had even started talking about going on a vacation together.

"So, have you made it official?" Nicole asked on one of our day-off lunches before her appointment at the clinic. We had gone to our favorite place near the Grind called Cap's, a small diner where we usually split dessert and talked about our woes.

"We're just letting things happen," I said, not feeling a care or trouble in the world as I dug my fork into my half of the massive slab of cheesecake.

She smiled at me, giving me the side-eye. "Well, I haven't ever seen you so happy and carefree. I think he's good for you. Either that or you've been smelling too many paint fumes."

"It's all him. I swear, I can't stop thinking about him, and even when I'm not with him, I feel like he's still with me."

She tapped the table right next to my cell phone. "That's because you haven't stopped texting him the entire time we've been sitting here."

I took my phone and put it away. "Sorry. He just wanted me to know that he and Puck are about to go grab some lunch."

"And how has his friend been doing since you're around a lot more often?"

"We try to sleep at my house a bit more often, but when Puck's around, we get along. I think he likes me."

She took a big bite from her half and then wiped her mouth. "And have you met his mother?"

I wagged my fork. "It's not that serious yet, but who knows. Maybe soon."

"What about your father? Have you thought about how you're going to get those two to meet?"

I felt an aching in my gut. It was the unsettled feeling only my father could give me. "I have tried not to think about him at all, but thanks for the reminder." I dropped my fork on the plate as my tummy continued to grumble.

She gave me an apologetic look. "Sorry, Hope. I really hate that you can't just be up-front with the man. I mean, you're in love, right? It's a big deal. You two might end up married. Then what will he say and do?"

I didn't want to think about it. My belly twisted in knots, and I felt a little light-headed and sick. "Excuse me," I said, getting up from the table.

I went to the bathroom and found myself squatting down in front of the nearest toilet. When I was finished being sick, I walked to the sink to wash my hands. I put a cold paper towel on the back of my neck and took a few deep breaths to regain my composure.

When I walked back out, Nicole was quiet, staring at me as if she'd seen a ghost as I slid into the booth with her.

"Did you just get sick? Your face is flushed, and you're really pale."

"Yes, I did. And I'll thank you again, not to bring up my D.A.D." I didn't even want to hear the word, so I spelled it out.

She leaned in across the table and whispered, "Are you sure it's your D.A.D. making you sick?"

"I'm pretty sure. I'm only sick when I think of how controlling he is and how I am going to have to tell him the truth about Chris and me eventually. I mean, I don't know what else it could be."

"You don't?" She gave me a blank look as if I should know better. "Have you and Chris been careful every time?"

"I have the implant, remember?" My father had insisted I get it before going to college.

"Yeah, but isn't it only effective for so many years? You already said your period was screwy. I told you that might mean there was a problem with that. I'd get a test and check it out. You can ask for one while we're at the clinic. Just to be sure."

"It's fine. It's just my dad. I'm stressing out about him. I told you he wanted me to come in for the holidays, and I know he's going to try and make me move back. He's got Aunt Mary's office chair ready and waiting. By then, I'll be done with school, so I can't use that as a reason."

"Well, it could be worse. You could not be a rich heiress to a big company. You know, like me?" She snorted a laugh and then took a drink of her soda.

"You know it's not as easy as all of that," I said, wishing I'd never told her anything about my inheritance. She was a good friend, but she liked to tease me relentlessly about it.

"Sorry, I know your nerves have always been bad, I just think you should pay attention to your body. And since we'll be there, why not?" She had always given me great advice, but I couldn't help but think she was overreacting.

"Because it's nothing. I listen to my body, and it usually starts to go haywire at the mention of you-know-who." I wasn't going to continue to talk about the old man. He had taken enough of my lunch.

As she finished off the dessert alone, I called for the check and paid the ticket. "You got last time," I said when she protested.

"Thank you," she said, not putting up as much of a fight as usual. "And, thank you for going down to the campus clinic with me."

"It's the least I can do. I hate going there too. The last time I went, I left with a handful of unwanted STD pamphlets."

"Was one of them about pregnancy?" she asked. I gave her a pointed look. "Hope. I'm serious. I'm a little worried about you. If you don't get that checked, at least get your stomach checked and tell them your stress symptoms. You could have an ulcer. It's not normal to have that kind of stress from anyone. Especially as often as you do."

"Fine. But only because I'm tired of letting him control me. If it is stress, then maybe I can tell him how bad it's gotten. Maybe he'll back off." Not a chance. My father would probably only get worse to put me down like he did my mother.

"Good. I'll feel better."

She finished her dessert while I sipped my soda, feeling

my stomach get back to normal. After we left, we drove to the campus and then went to the clinic.

"What are you going to do if you are pregnant?" she asked me.

"I'm not pregnant. I think you're right about the ulcer. It's been going on for a while, long before Chris ever came into my life."

"Maybe, maybe not." She signed in and then wrote my name below hers.

"Are you sure I don't need an appointment?"

"It's fine. They see every student. They'll just squeeze you in." We sat together, and a moment later, she was passing me a pregnancy pamphlet. Then the receptionist called us, one by one, to get our paperwork so we could sign in.

After filling out the forms and bringing them back to the front, Nicole was called to the back. She had gotten a UTI over a week ago, and none of the over-the-counter meds were working.

I sat waiting quietly while another young lady was called in ahead of me, but after her, I heard my name.

"Hope Mayhew." The nurse stood with her clipboard, wearing dark purple scrubs and a tired expression. "Come back here with me. I'm Gretta, and we're going to see what we can do for you. What brings you in today?"

"Well, my friend thinks I'm pregnant, but I have been having stress issues for a while now. So, she insisted I come. I think it's an ulcer."

"What kind of stress has you that upset?" Gretta asked. "Studies?"

"No, ma'am. It's my father. He's driving me crazy."

She shook her head. "For me, it's my mother. She had me so upset a few years ago; I broke out into hives. I distanced myself for a year, went back home, and boom, we're inseparable."

"My mother is dead," I said, not trying to kill Gretta's mood. "But I think if she were around, it would be a lot better."

"Well, let's get some blood drawn. It's the sure way to tell what's wrong. Have you had unprotected sex?" She gave me a scrutinous look.

"I've been seeing this guy," I said. It wasn't like I was sleeping around with multiple partners.

Gretta gave a soft laugh. "So have 99.9 percent of women who end up with an STD, Hope. I'll be sure to give you some condoms when you leave."

"That's not necessary," I said. "I can buy some. As for pregnancy, I don't think it is that, because I have the implant."

"Oh? When did you get it?"

"The summer before my freshman year. My dad's idea of a graduation gift. He didn't want me to get knocked up. So, it's been just over three years."

She shook her head. "Those devices are only really good for three years, give or take a few months." She gave me a sympathetic look. "Take the freebies. If we don't give them out, they expire, and then we just have to throw them away."

She let out a long breath, then put the blood pressure cuff on me. Next, a thermometer appeared from her cart, and then she handed it to me. "Under the tongue." She had me done in no time, and then she walked out of the room and returned with a few packages.

One contained a plastic cup. "Go in that bathroom there and fill this up. We'll do a test while I take your blood. It will let us know more about this stress issue, and I can see if you're fighting off an infection. Then I'll know how to treat you."

I took the cup, and when I returned, she walked over and popped the sterile strip into the urine.

"Now, that can work its magic while we fill these tubes." She prepared the needle and then swabbed my arm. A moment later, she was filling the tubes, and finally, I was done. The needle was removed, and I could breathe a sigh of relief.

"So, when will that test be ready?" I asked, glancing across the room to the sample.

She picked it up and then held the strip out. I tried to read her expression, but she had a very strong poker face.

"It's positive. You're pregnant, honey. I'll call you later to let you know about the results from your bloodwork. But I have a feeling that any recent stress sickness is morning sickness, so you might want to do what you have to do to make sure you stay away from anything that will stress you out too much. Like your father, for example."

I was shocked. How was I supposed to hide this from my father? He was going to be livid. I felt my stomach roll again, and I barely made it to the garbage can before I vomited.

"Here, have a seat, honey." The nurse helped me into a chair. "You just sit tight and catch your breath. Has that happened in the past few mornings?"

"It happened a couple of mornings ago, but I thought that was just because my dad had texted me. I mean, he doesn't really bother me so much all of the time, it's just some of the time."

"Well, you need to take it easy. For you and that baby."

I waited another minute, and when I walked out into

the lobby to find Nicole waiting, and I burst into tears. "You were right," I said.

"Oh, Hope. It's going to be okay once the shock wears off. It's a little baby, and babies are everything."

"I'm sorry, Nicole. I just don't know how I feel right now. I feel a bit numb."

"Well, you need to go and see Chris. Talk it out, and you'll figure it out together." She wrapped her arms around me and gave me comfort. I would need it for what I had to do.

CHAPTER 15

As the day went on, Puck and I returned from lunch and a bit of ax throwing for his evening appointment. As we walked into the shop, where the other artists were busy doing tattoos, including Puck's apprentice, who was working on a friend's back, I glanced at my phone, wondering why it had been so quiet.

I knew Hope had gone to the doctor with her friend, and I had given her a little time to do so, but it seemed like I would hear something already.

"Still no response?" Puck asked, who had a look of concern on his face as well. "I'm sure it's nothing. They probably just went out shopping after the appointment. You know women, always wanting to spend money."

"Yeah."

"So, where do you two stand? Are you official yet?" He sat on the stool beside me.

"We haven't really talked about it. Which is why I can't really freak out on her for ignoring me. I mean, we spend a lot of time together, but we've never really talked about what happens next. It's like we just live in the moment. We've agreed that we want to see what happens, but as far as making anything official. Nope. It hasn't happened."

"Do you think she would suddenly come to her senses and change her mind about you?" he tried to tease.

"I don't know, but now I'm starting to worry."

"Don't freak out. She's probably just charging her phone or some shit. You should wait a bit. Give them a few hours. They're women on the town." He waggled his brows at me. "Maybe they went out for drinks?"

I walked up the stairs, and then on my way to the apartment, I found Hope sitting in the stairwell.

"Hey, you. What the hell happened? I've been calling and texting all afternoon. I was getting worried about you."

"Us. There's no me anymore," she mumbled, looking shell-shocked.

She was right. We were us, not just the two of us, but one unit. At least we'd been acting as such. Maybe she already saw us together, as a couple. "Yeah, I wanted to talk about that. I know we haven't exactly figured out what we're doing, but—"

She passed me a plastic baggie with something inside. "What's this?" I asked, feeling her hand on my arm. I looked at her and realized she'd been crying. "Hey, let's go inside." I took her by the hand, thinking this all had something to do with her father. And as soon as I figured out what the baggie was, the better. "What is this about?"

I walked her to the apartment, unlocked the door, and we went inside before she took a deep breath and told me.

"It's a pregnancy test," she said, walking over to the window. "I took a test today after getting sick at lunch. I'm pregnant, Chris."

My face felt numb. I wasn't sure what to think. It was

my understanding that she had some fancy, expensive birth control device that meant she couldn't get pregnant. We had talked about it after the first time we were together. I even looked it up and read about it. How had this happened?

"Say something," she said. "Are you angry?"

"No way, I'm just—it's sudden, you know? I thought you were covered."

"I thought so too," she said, sniffling. She looked down, and I wondered if she had tears in her eyes.

"It's going to be okay."

"I don't know that. My dad is going to cut me off, and I'll have no money to pay for having a baby, much less will I be able to take care of one."

"I'll help you in any way I can." She seemed so distant. "We'll get through this."

"I'm not sure what I'm going to do," she said.

"Oh, I see." It seemed like it should be a no-brainer with me in the picture. I mean, I was in it, right? I leaned against the kitchen cabinets and wondered what she was going to do, and if she was going to consider me at all.

She wrapped her arms around her belly. "I didn't expect it, Chris. I don't want you to think I was trying to trap you or anything. I mean, I don't expect anything from you."

"Well, why not? I mean, you should, right? *I* expect something from me. This is my baby too." I didn't understand why she would just assume I didn't want any part of its life, but I had to respect the fact that it was her body and her choice. "What do you want me to do?"

"I don't know. I guess just be patient for a while."

"I can do that, as I stand here on my ear, trying to let it soak in."

She gave a nervous laugh. "I hear you. I think that's why the nurse gave me the strip. She knew it would be hard to accept."

Her shoulders drew in as she leaned against the window, resting her forehead on the frame. She looked so small, and all I could do was go to her, pull her into my arms, and make sure that she knew I cared. So I did just that.

She collapsed against me. "Oh, Chris. I don't know what to do."

"Have you ever thought about having children?"

"I thought I would someday. Maybe when we got a bit older, settled in a little, you know? Did all of the things we want to do in life. That would be fine, but right now? I'm not ready. Are you?"

"I could get used to the idea. I just want you to know that I'll be here for you no matter what you choose." It was the right thing to say, or so I thought. It wasn't like I had dealt with anything like it before.

"Come on," I said. "Let's get you off of your feet." I led her over to the couch and sat down, pulling her onto my lap. I kissed her cheek and stroked her hair. As much as I knew it was a scary situation for her, I kind of liked the idea of being a dad. Yeah, it wasn't exactly how I had planned it, but it was a sweet surprise.

I could see the two of us together, raising a child and nurturing it. We could rent the entire building and build a home for our son or daughter to be raised in.

My heart warmed a bit, thinking of a little dark-haired girl. She would have her mother's smile and eyes, and of course, a piece of my heart. Or a son who would grow up strong and handsome. No matter boy or girl, with parents like us, both would be talented enough to make a difference in the world.

"It may not be as bad as you think."

"How am I going to raise a child with a job at Paddy's and no degree without going back home to New York when my dad kills my allowance because of this?"

"I know it's your body, but I want this baby. It's mine too."

"I'm having the baby, Chris. I just don't know what happens next, okay?"

It was perfectly clear. I stood up. "So, you don't know if you want to stay here with me, then. Is that it? You're not really into us being an us?" I was the only one she was rejecting.

"I don't know, and it doesn't matter what I want anymore. I have my child to worry about, and I can't make it in the city without my family's money when it's just me. How can I take care of a baby too?"

"You act like I'm not here for you at all. I am the baby's father, and in case you didn't notice, I'm actually not as disappointed as you must think I was going to be." I took a deep breath, trying to control my tone. I didn't want to yell at the mother of my child, and I didn't want to upset her. "You're not even considering my feelings."

"I'm sorry. I just thought—"

"You thought wrong if you thought I was going to just turn my back on my family. That's my child. My blood." I found myself getting loud again, so I turned and went up the stairs. Once at the top, I closed my eyes and tried to take a few deep breaths. I had never let her see this side of me, and I wasn't about to let her now.

I looked down into the living room to find her leaving. I

knew I had to go after her. I hurried down the stairs and then ran out into the stairwell.

She turned around with tears in her eyes. "I'm scared," she said, loud enough for Puck to get up and close the tattoo parlor door. She covered her face, embarrassed that she was making a scene. "I'm sorry."

"Dammit, Hope. The first thing you have to do is stop apologizing. Please." I pulled her close and held her tightly. "I'm not going anywhere. We're in this together."

"But we're not. I'm the one who has to have this baby. I'm not sure I can be a mother, but maybe someone else can." Those words were gut-wrenching. "And I'm sorry," she continued. "But I wanted us to figure it out before we had something like this forcing us together."

"Do you not want to be with me?" I pulled away and cupped her face, looking into her eyes. "If you don't want me, say so."

She let out a long breath. "I don't know what I want, Chris. I guess I just need time alone to think." She turned and hurried down the stairs, nearly giving me a heart attack in the process. Not only was she leaving me hanging, but she could have tripped down the damned stairs.

I had the overwhelming feeling to protect her and felt utterly useless as she got in her car and sped away.

CHAPTER 16

HOPE

It had been nearly a week since I left the tattoo parlor, unclear of what would come next in my life. As I lay in my bed, feeling sorry for myself after a long, early shift at Paddy's, I had come to the conclusion that adoption might be the answer. It was something I kept thinking about. Mostly because I was just so young, and I wasn't ready. Chris had his entire life to live as well. I still had so much to do, and I couldn't bring a child into my father's life. He had already ruined mine, and I hated to think of how he'd treat my kid. The son or daughter of an artist. He would never see Chris for what he considered to be a 'real man.' Chris being loving and kind to his daughter wouldn't matter to him in the least.

It was just so much to think about, which was hard on me since it also made my stomach hurt. After a few days, I'd determined what pains were the pregnancy, and which were from the ulcer, which, as the test results proved, I did have.

I had to be extra calm, cool, and collected in order to

keep my stress levels low. And with the baby as a new incentive, I was doing better.

I was sitting on my bed, staring at my phone, when Nicole called. "Hey, girl," she said. "I'm on my way up." She had been out of town the past two days with her mother, and now she was back, and I couldn't be happier to see her.

"The door is open." I buzzed her up and then went to the kitchen to fix us a couple of drinks, the ones I could safely have at least.

Two minutes later, she was standing in my living room, taking off her shoes, which she always did as soon as she hit my door. She dropped her purse on the couch and joined me in the kitchen. "How are you doing?"

"I'm good."

"And the baby?"

"Still the size of a grain of rice last time I checked."

"Well, it's a start. And I'm sure it's going to be the best baby ever for its godmother."

"Nicole. I need to talk to you about that. Do you think I should keep the baby or give it up for someone else to raise? Someone who can give it a better life."

"That's the dumbest thing I've ever heard. You're an heiress, with money, and you have a boyfriend who is so worried about you that he's started calling me."

"I don't want him to only choose me because of a baby. I mean, he deserves happiness too."

"And I'm pretty sure by the way he's been blowing up my phone that he thinks you and that baby *are* his happiness." She poked at my phone, which was lying on the kitchen counter where I had put it so I could ignore it. "He doesn't understand why you just ghosted him, and honestly, neither do I."

"I'm just so confused," I said, breaking down in tears. I laid my head on the counter, and Nicole ran around to comfort me.

"Call him, will you? You two need to talk. He's there for you. It's more than you can say about most men, at least in my experience. And it's not like you're all alone."

"I just want to make the best decision for the baby."

"Well, what if—and now just hear me out for a minute, because I've had crazier ideas—but what if you and Chris raised the baby together as loving parents? I mean, for one, it's your child; you'd know it and understand it better than anyone else can. Unless you don't ever want to be a mother."

"Of course I do. I want all of that. I just hate to think of subjecting it to my father."

"Look, Hope. You've got to stop letting your father dictate everything that happens. You're a grown woman Hope. You're letting him drive away a man who loves you, the father of your child, mind you. And for what? Because he's going to take away some money that you won't need in another six years anyway? Have you ever looked at the stipulations of your trust? Or did you just take dear old dad's word for it?"

"What do you mean?"

"Well, how do you know that your mother didn't make special clauses for you. I know it's possible. You should check into it."

I had never really thought about it before. "What should I do about Chris? He hates him."

"I'm sure Chris is a big boy, and I bet you he can take care of himself against your father. He might even be able to protect you. I know one thing: he'd sure like to try."

"He talked to you a lot, didn't he?" I could imagine the two of them and all they'd have to say about me.

"For nearly two hours. You have to call him."

I picked up my phone and then walked over to the couch, where I eased back and tucked my feet up beside me. "I'm going to do it." I stared at the phone. "Maybe we could drive over there instead? I just feel like the things I have to say might be better in person?" I took a deep breath and gave her a pleading look. "I'll drive."

She thought a moment. "No, I had better drive. Just in case you decide to stay."

About forty minutes later, we were pulling up at the tattoo parlor, and I showed her where to park in the back. "I use the back entrance."

"Cool. So, does it go to the tattoo parlor?"

"Yes. Come on in. You will love this place. I just hope that Chris is glad to see me."

"He will be, trust me." She got out, and I followed, leading her to the door.

I opened the back entrance and walked inside, peeking into the tattoo parlor before going upstairs, just to see what was going on. Puck looked up from his station, and his eyes went straight to Nicole's. "Hey, ladies. How can I help you?" I looked down and saw that the man he was tattooing was Chris. And there was a young girl standing at his side, rubbing his shoulders.

He glanced up and spotted me in the mirror and then shrugged her off. "Thanks, Mina."

She walked away, and when she stopped to look back at me, she turned and hurried back to the other station, where she sat down beside one of the other artists. I wasn't sure what was going on, but by the daggers I shot her, everyone knew that I wasn't happy about it.

Chris sat up. "Puck, this is Nicole. Nicole, my best friend, Puck." He still hadn't said anything to me, and I felt as if I may cry about the time he stood up and walked over to offer me his hand. "Come on, Hope. Let's go upstairs."

Had he changed his mind? Was the girl his new muse? She had short hair like mine in blueberry black and enough tats of her own to join the circus.

I reluctantly followed, wondering if he was going to let me down easy.

But when we got in the stairwell, he turned around and pulled me close, kissing me hard and deep. He pulled away. "I just had to do that again."

"Who was the girl?" I asked.

"Oh, that's Royal's girl. He's the other artist, and she was just helping me out with a cramp. Puck hit a nerve, and I tensed up."

"I see."

"I called Nicole."

"I know. She told me."

"Don't be mad; I just needed to talk to someone who really knows you." He looked me up and down. "God, I've missed you so much. You're so beautiful it hurts."

He had always said the sweetest things. And what made it better was how he spoke from his heart. "I missed you. And I'm sorry."

"What did I tell you about that? You don't owe me an apology." He looked up the stairs. "Come on, let's go up."

I followed him up to the apartment, and when we were inside, he offered me a seat as if it were the first time I'd been there. "I'm ready to talk and figure this out."

"Look, Hope. I just need to say my piece, okay?" He searched my eyes, and I gave a nod as my eyes welled up with tears.

"Go ahead."

He moved to sit beside me and pulled me in close. "Stop crying. I can't stand to see you cry." He kissed my forehead and then met my eyes. "I want you and me to be more. I want us to have this baby, raise it, and love it."

"Are you sure? Have you really thought about it? It's not going to be easy, and it will change everything."

"Yes, I have thought about it. And it's for the better. It doesn't change the fact that I want to be with you. I wanted that before I knew about the baby. It's just now we'll have a little part of ourselves to share and love with each other."

"I agree. I want to keep it too. I mean, abortion was never an option, but I just thought maybe someone else would make a better mother than me."

"*You're* the best mother for our baby. And I'm going to make sure I prove that to you every single day." He kissed me hard, and soon, I felt as if I might just melt into a puddle.

"I'm scared," I said, thinking of my father.

"I know. But I'll be with you the whole way."

"It's not that, I mean, yes, I'm afraid of all of that, like something going wrong, or something hurting the baby, but I mean my father. I can't help but wonder what the hell is going to happen when he finds out. He's going to cut me off. I just know it."

"So what? I don't need his money to make sure my family has everything they need. I'll get an extra job and do all I can to make sure you have the best care, and that you and our child never go without."

I kissed him hard, our bodies falling together eagerly as the knock came to the door. "Shit, I can't believe I bailed on Nicole."

"It's cool. I'm sure Puck kept her busy."

Another bang came to the door. "Open up, you love-birds. We want to go get a bite to eat."

"I could eat," I said.

"Hold your horses, dammit," Chris said. He got up and went over to open the door.

Puck strolled in with his arm around Nicole. "You two really should slow it down. The next thing you know, Hope's going to end up pregnant. Oh, wait. Too late!"

"You're not funny." Chris put his arm around me, and then we left the apartment, going down to the Grind. "I guess this is our first official double date," he said.

We walked down the street to the Grind, where Puck showed Nicole his favorite food truck, and she introduced him to the one he had been reluctant to try.

Meanwhile, Hope and I had gone to buy more sweet bacon bao buns. "Split the fries with me?" she asked, giving me a sweet smile.

"Our kid is in trouble," I mumbled, then turned to the man in the window. "Go ahead and give us a large order of sweet and hot fries too, please."

"Why? They aren't that spicy," she said, giving me a nudge. I hoped they didn't bother her ulcer, but she knew more about what affected her than me.

"No, I mean me. I already find it hard to tell you no, and I know it's going to be damned near impossible to tell him no too."

"Him? You can't be so sure of that. It could be a little girl." She laced her fingers with mine.

The man handed me the order, and we carried our food over to the sitting area where we saved places for Puck and

Nicole, who were on their way to their second truck. "Well, in that case, I'm really screwed. She's going to be ruined from the moment I see her."

She leaned into me, resting her head on my shoulder. "We're going to be parents, Chris. Are you really ready for it?"

I opened up my order and then helped her with hers. "I can't wait."

"The more I think about it, I'm kind of getting excited. I've always wondered what my children will look like."

I had thought about that too. "I keep picturing this little girl with dark hair. She's beautiful. So, no pink hair until she's twenty," I said, teasing her.

"No pink hair ever," she said, popping one of the fries into her mouth.

I laughed and nodded. "Yes. No pink hair ever."

"Look at those two," she said, leaning into me. "I can't believe you told her about Puck. But it makes sense."

"Well, she's a nice girl, and a knockout like her best friend, and well, Puck deserves someone. He's put up with me for long enough."

"What does he think about the baby?" she asked, with genuine concern in her eyes that made me realize how special she really was. She not only cared about me but my friend too.

"Are you kidding? He's ecstatic. He wants to be called Uncle Puck. He said he might even buy the two of them a coonskin cap like in that John Candy movie. He's going to be a handful."

"The baby or Puck?" she asked with a laugh.

"Both," I chuckled. "I can't wait for birthday parties, and Christmas, and—"

"Shit," she said, shrinking back from me. "Christmas. I

know it's a way off, but my father expects me to come back to New York for the holidays. I can't keep this from him for too long."

I had already thought about that. While she had me on hold, wondering if we were going to even be together again, I thought about how much control her father had over her and what I'd like to say to the man. I wasn't afraid of him. And I wasn't going to let him bully her anymore. "I don't think you should keep it from him. It's not like we can change what happened, and it's not like it's a horrible thing. We're in love, and we're having a baby."

"You love me?"

"Of course. Don't you love me?"

"Yeah, it's just I've never heard you say it. I mean, neither one of us has said it."

"I was going to talk to you about us and tell you how I felt when you told me you were pregnant. I had talked it out in my mind that entire day, and I just needed to know something for sure. Even though I guess I already felt that way all along."

"I know what you mean. It's like we just fit together, and it all made sense. Maybe someone knew that we were meant for each other."

"All I know is, I don't ever want you to leave me again."

"Me either," Nicole said, coming up behind him. "Sorry, I wasn't eavesdropping."

"She totally was," said Puck. "And so was I." He reached over and stole one of our fries and then sat down with Nicole across from us.

"Okay, so maybe I was. What can I do? I am who I am. But this one, he was so down in the dumps, I swear, I nearly called you myself and begged you to take him back."

"You didn't have to live with him," Puck added. "He

hasn't painted for days. I caught him walking around like a zombie. He turned to me and said, 'All of the rainbows are gone."

Hope belted a laugh, holding her hand over her tummy as if instinctively knowing our child was in there. "Did you really?"

"No. One thing you'll learn about Puck is he's a filthy liar." I looked at Nicole as I said it. "So, be careful."

"It's called teasing, dammit." He turned to Nicole. "Do not listen to a word that man says. I promise you, he's mental. In fact, it might carry over to the kid."

"Hey now, leave my kid out of it," I said. "It's barely a peanut, and you're already making fun of him."

"You're already sounding like a square," he continued. "Thank goodness the kid will have his dear Uncle Puck around to teach him the hard lessons in life. I can give him his first tattoo and take him to drink his first beer."

"Easy, now. If I have a girl, you're not touching her with a tattoo gun, or I'll murder you."

"If you have a girl, I'll help you hide the bodies of anyone who tries to date her before she's thirty."

Hope and Nicole exchanged a look. "First of all, you will have to get through me. I'm going to be the Godmother, so I'll say where we hide the bodies."

"Oh, yes, ma'am." Puck waggled his brows. "I like her. She's vicious like me." He put his arm around her and then fed her one of his chips.

They seemed to be a perfect fit, and while I wasn't sure what would happen between them, I hoped they realized they would have to be in each other's lives for a long time and not do anything to make that too uncomfortable to bear.

"I'm not sure if I should finish school," Hope said, the subject popping up out of nowhere.

"What?"

"I'm not sure I'll be able to afford it. Not with my father making it hard for me."

"I told her to check into her mother's trust. There were bound to be clauses in place," Nicole chimed in.

Nicole was a smart woman, but I wondered why Hope wouldn't know the stipulations of her trust. "Have you ever spoken to a lawyer?"

"No. My father handles all of that."

"Well, I think it's time you did. You should make sure he's not just setting rules to suit himself. I know Puck and I are joking about our little girl, but it's quite possible that he's just being overprotective. I'm already feeling protective of you and the baby, and we've got a long way until it's here."

"It would sure solve a lot of my problems," she said.

"Look, either way, you're not quitting school. You have a trust allowance that he can't touch. Use that for your school and let me take care of everything else."

"It's not going to be easy." She closed her eyes and then rested her head on my shoulder.

"Well, you never know. I did get a call from Virginia earlier, and it seems that I have someone interested in the museum piece."

"Do you think it will sell?" she asked, so surprised that she grabbed my arm and squeezed it tightly.

"Yes, and I've already arranged for you to have a nice big portion of the profit. I wanted to thank you for your inspiration."

She sank back a bit, her shoulders slumping. "You didn't have to do that because of what my father said." She covered her mouth, and I could tell she was embarrassed.

"It's not because of your father. And I will still make out

like a bandit if the deal goes through. Besides, it's good business."

"Well, thank you. But I'm still chewing on the whole school thing. I'm going to be a mother. And besides that, I have my whole life to go back and get that degree."

I hated that she felt like she had to give up anything. "You can do it all. Anything. I have faith in you."

She smiled big and then ate another fry. "This is so good," she said, but I knew it was to change the subject.

"Try this," Nicole said, passing her a portion of her sandwich she hadn't touched. "It's to die for."

We spent the rest of the time at the Grind eating and chatting, and then we went back to the house where we sat in the living room playing Scrabble. We had a good time, and even though I was pretty sure Puck was making up words, I let it slide. The ladies found him charming, especially Nicole, who couldn't take her eyes off him.

"You should let him do your tattoo," Hope said. "You've been talking about it for four years now."

"And I'll probably think about it for four more before I do it." She shook her head. "Besides, I'm not sure I want that anymore. There are so many new ideas."

"Let me know, and I'll hook you up," Puck said. "I will give you the family discount, seeing as we're family."

"Puck is the best in the city. He's going to do a show pretty soon. We'll all have to go out to support him." I liked the idea of having someone to do things with. She enriched my life in ways she'd never understand.

"You could get your baby bump tattooed," Nicole said with a laugh.

"No, she can't," I said. "Pregnant mothers can't go under our needles. It's our shop's policy."

"Yeah, because we don't want any babies coming out

with face tats," Puck said, earning a laugh from the two ladies. I'd heard it many times before. Puck didn't have a lot of new material, or maybe I'd just lived with him too long.

As I watched Hope laughing, I felt like everything was perfect in the world. Her happiness was mine.

I sat on the counter in his kitchen, watching him make eggs at the stove feet away from me. I hadn't intended on sitting there until he hefted me up, kissing me madly when I entered the room. "I've been thinking," I said, taking a deep breath.

"I thought I felt the earth shake," Puck said, who had come up for breakfast after spending another night on the downstairs couch. Nicole had gone home sometime in the night, and I wasn't sure how close the two had gotten, but Puck seemed to be in a happy mood.

"Hey, watch it, that's the mother of my child you're teasing," he said, rolling up a towel to pop him with.

Puck chuckled. "Aw, is someone a protective father already? Your kid is going to like me better anyway." He grabbed a coffee cup as I cleared my throat dramatically.

"Excuse me. I have a very important announcement," I said, tapping the counter with a wooden spoon I'd found beside me. "May I have your attention?"

"Attention granted," Puck said.

Chris laughed. "I'm listening."

"I've decided I'm definitely going to finish school." I hoped it would ease his mind. "But with the baby coming and our decision to remain together, I feel we need to figure out some sort of game plan."

Puck finished making his cup of coffee and turned from the counter. "That's my cue. This is way too serious for me."

When he was gone, I waited for Chris's response. He nodded, cracking an egg into the pan. "Actually, I'd wanted to talk to you about that. I don't want you to quit school either."

"Well, I'm going to need a different job, that's for sure. Especially when my father figures out that I'm going to have a baby." I dreaded telling him anything.

"Your father is going to have to accept it. What's done is done, and we're both happy. He can't control the universe. Especially ours."

"I've been trying to figure out if I should keep the apartment or find a different one."

"We'll find one together. I don't want you living alone, and it feels like the next step." He turned his eyes up to me. "Do you agree?"

I had hoped he would suggest living together. "Yes, I do. I'm glad I brought it up."

"Me too, and I'm happy about school."

"Did you ever hear anything else about the sale of the painting?"

He gave a bleak look. "Not yet, and I honestly haven't ever seen a deal take this long. It's not like Virginia to keep me in the dark either, which has me a bit worried. It's times like this where I wish I had an agent."

"You should hire one." I hopped down off the counter.

"Careful," he said, stepping away from the eggs. "Don't fall."

"Relax. I've hardly become that delicate." I gave him a kiss. "I just wanted some juice." I opened the door of the fridge to find two jugs of juice.

"Don't drink the one labeled Malibu, it's got rum in it. Puck mixes it now and then."

I spotted the jug of orange that had a duct tape label with MALIBU written in bold, black letters. "Noted. No rum." At least he had labeled it. That would have been a big surprise.

Chris cleared his throat, and it was as if something was weighing on his mind as he spoke. "You know, I was thinking about something last night. I mean, it's a long shot, because I know you probably have a better plan, but what if *you* were my agent?"

"Me?" I tried to think of a reason I couldn't be his agent, and nothing came to mind. I was capable and had managed more before working at Paddy's. "Are you sure?" I didn't know if it was a smart idea to work together. I didn't want him to hate the job I was doing and have it cause problems.

"You would get to use your business degree."

"Which I haven't quite earned."

"But still, you're almost done, right?"

"I have half a semester left, sure. I was short a few credits due to personal stress, but come Christmas I'll be done. That's why my father wants me to move home."

"Well, that's not happening. You're going to stay here with me, and we're going to find an amazing apartment and have our baby. You working for me as an agent will give us the life we want; you'll manage my business, work my negotiations, and I can handle the rest. Then we'll have all the time we want together."

I poured a glass of juice and then went to sit at the small table. "Are you sure you want to move?"

"I can lease the apartment to Puck. He's slept on the couch long enough to afford it, and it's right here above his shop. Besides, we could use the extra income." He finished cooking the eggs and took the toast from the oven.

He walked over to the table and put the plate between us. Then he handed me a fork. "See? It's all going to work out. Besides, with you managing my art, you'll work your best to get us a better negotiation and more money. We'll have total control over our lives."

"Speaking of total control," I said, stabbing my fork into the slice of toast. "I thought about taking Nicole's advice and doing a little digging into my trust. It's hard to believe my mother had something so strict setup. But then, it may be true. After all, Dad is an asshole. So, he probably forced her into the stipulations. He knew she wasn't well."

"I think it's smart. You need to at least know what it says, and if he's being honest, which I find a little hard to believe, based on the way he treats you, then at least you'll know that too."

"I should have checked already, but I know if he finds out I'm looking into it behind his back, he's going to be upset."

"Is the trust in your name?" he asked, spooning some egg onto his toast and folding it in half. "If it's in your name, and he's not in control of it, then he can't keep you from it."

"He's been in the advertising business so long. He knows everyone. He's got connections."

"Well, I think you should contact a lawyer from here and have them look into it."

"I don't know any lawyers here."

"Not yet, but I would like for you to meet my mother. I mean, it was in the works already, but this gives us a good reason."

"I'm not sure it's the best way to meet her. What do I do or say? Hello, I'm carrying your grandchild, and I have a shitload of family issues?"

He reached across the table to take my hand. "I'm sure it will be fine. She's heard worse. Besides, knowing the mother of her grandchild is a trust fund kid isn't the worst news ever."

I couldn't help but laugh. "You just love me for my trust fund, don't you?"

"As much as you love me for my gallery commission." He gave me a wink.

"I don't love you for your talent; I love you for the sex." I couldn't even say it without laughing, but before I knew it, he was on his knees in front of me, kissing me like a sex-crazed maniac.

"Now, there's something we can make plans for. What are you doing for the next few hours?"

"I've got to go to work." I hated having to be responsible.

"Ten minutes?" He pawed at me, cupping my breast as he kissed my neck and squeezed my knee, which sent chills down my spine and tickled me more than expected.

I giggled, squirming away from him. "Stop it! I can't be late."

"I'll talk to Jude," he said as his phone rang.

"Oh? Will you? I don't think that will work."

He got up and found his phone across the room on the counter. "It's my mother. Let's see if she's interested in meeting up to talk about this. Maybe a late dinner?" He answered the phone and then leaned against the counter. "Hey, Mom."

I felt a slight wave of nausea but pushed through it and ate the toast. But it was the egg that got me, and I ran out of the kitchen to the bathroom where I rejected everything I'd put in my tummy.

Chris came to the door a minute later. "My mother said she'd love to meet you and talk about your trust."

As soon as he said the words, I turned and vomited again.

He came over and rubbed my back. "She gives me that reaction at times too," he said teasing. "Are you okay?"

"Yes, it was the eggs. I guess they got me."

"Yolks or the whole thing?"

I nodded. "Maybe the yolks."

"Next time, we'll try them without. You should try to eat another piece of toast. Or at least some crackers." He stroked my hair, pulling it back from my face. "Come on, I'll get you something."

"I still have to go to work. Morning sickness is no excuse." And I knew he was just trying to get me to stay so that eventually he could get me into bed. It was tempting, but I had a future to think about.

"Come on, take the job with me instead." I could hear the plea in his voice, and it was hard not to jump into it with both feet just to make him happy.

But I knew it was a big decision, and I couldn't act in haste. "I have to think about it, Chris. I can't just leave Paddy's hanging anyway. I'd have to put in a notice, or at least make sure the job is going to pay out first."

He groaned, his shoulders slumping. "I have faith in you," he said, still encouraging me.

I got to my feet and followed him out of the bathroom and into the kitchen, where he passed me another piece of toast.

I took it and bit it. "I'll think about it. I'll let you know later, okay?"

"Fine, but I am taking you to meet my mother when you get home from work. She said we can pop in or meet her for dinner. I told her I'd be in touch."

I took a deep breath. "Okay. I'll have to prepare myself for that. Do we have to tell her I'm pregnant yet?"

"She's going to find out sooner than later, and maybe you can practice for when you tell your dad."

"It's not going to happen anytime soon. I can't deal with the stress." There was only so much I could take. I bit into the toast and let it ease my stomach.

"I agree anyway. But we can't wait forever, Hope. We'll find out about this trust, and then you can talk to him."

"By then, he'll know something's up." I closed my eyes and tried to relax, not wanting to upset my ulcer. "I feel I have to warn you, Chris. It's going to get a lot worse before it gets better where my father is concerned."

"Well, you should know that I'm worried about your father."

"Good, that's makes one of us." He was only worried because he had no idea the horrors that awaited. "Welcome to my family."

CHAPTER 19

CHRIS

I walked up to my mother's house about the same time Virginia called. I stopped on the front doorstep and took a deep breath. My pulse quickened as I answered. "Hello, Virginia. Good news, I hope?" I had been waiting to hear back from her about the sale of my painting.

She hesitated a moment. "No, I'm sorry. I couldn't seal the deal. They just weren't interested in paying what we needed to get."

"How much was the offer?" I had a feeling that she was just being picky. She was always more concerned with her commission than making a sale.

"He offered twenty-six, but I thought you should at least get thirty. You don't want to start undercutting yourself, and that thing was eighteen canvases."

"Yes, and not one of them is worth a damned thing without the complete set. We talked about pricing it to sell, Virginia. It's a large piece with special placing since it's a grouping. It's going to be hard to find the right customer."

I wondered if she had just blown any chance the art would sell.

"Calm down, now, Chris. I know what I'm doing. I've been in this business a lot longer, and for the size alone, I know I've made the right decision."

I took a deep breath, knowing I needed to do something about my representation. Even if Hope didn't take the job, I was going to have to find someone who could take care of those deals. Virginia was only out for herself and the gallery. She didn't care that I had needs. "Look, I don't want this to drag out. I need the money."

"Are you in some kind of trouble? You sound desperate."

"No, I'm not. But I have a life, Virginia. I have bills to pay, and quite frankly, I'd like some income before I run out of money from the last work that sold."

"Then I suggest you get to painting. I have inquiries all the time about your work. Do a smaller piece, maybe a few single canvases for a change. No one told you to do eighteen!" She was losing her cool, but she always did when she was called out.

I thought of the other pieces I had. "You know I have stuff in my private collection. Have you given them my card or sent them to my website or Instagram?"

"I have told them that you have other work, yes. But they all want this pink girl."

"I have more. I'll get it uploaded. And Virginia, I'm in talks with an agent. Someone I really hope will work out for me, so I just wanted to give you a heads-up."

"I appreciate that, although you know I don't mind handling your affairs, Christian."

"I'm aware, but I have to get something sold. I have a lot going on."

"Okay, well, there was one other call. He sounded interested and left his number. I wasn't quick to get back with him, because he was a bit rude and well, we already had one bite, but perhaps now that this one has fallen through, I'll give him a call."

"I'd appreciate that."

"Unless you'd rather wait for your agent to come on board?" Her tone was bitter, as expected. She didn't want to lose her cut.

"No, Virginia, just see what happens." I couldn't help but raise my voice, and my mother opened the door about the time I hung up.

"Who are you yelling at out here?" She stepped aside, and I walked into her house. It was a modest home, and there were some parts that she hadn't remodeled. It was her canvas, her work of art.

"It was Virginia. She lost another sale. I think it's time I hired an agent, and actually, you'll get to meet her tonight."

"The girlfriend?" She made a face. "Oh, honey. That's a horrible idea. What if you break up? What if she rips you off? You know I see it every single day in court. Relationships and business don't mix."

"Well, this would be more of a family business, I'm hoping."

My mother's jaw fell open, and her eyes widened. "You mean you've finally found the one?"

"Yes, she's definitely that."

"Well, if she's so special, where is she? Why didn't you come together?" She walked over and poured herself a drink. "Do you want one?" she offered.

"No, thanks. And she's on her way. I had to give her the address because she's coming straight from work. And I want you to be on your best behavior."

"Aren't I always? I give as much respect as I get."

"Well, if you're not nice to her, you'll live to regret it. She's special."

"I get it. Now, will you just trust me and relax. Where did you meet her? And why am I just learning of this special woman?"

I knew she'd think I was deliberately trying to hide Hope from her. But in truth, my mother was the one with the busy schedule that prevented her from knowing as much as she wanted to know. "You shouldn't have left my art exhibit early. You would have met her. She was the subject of my painting."

"*The Girl with the Pink Hair?*" She narrowed her eyes. "You mean you're dating your model?"

"Yes, she's made me very happy and is an inspiration. I've painted her multiple times."

"Is that what you're calling it?" she said, rolling her eyes. "And you think that she's qualified to be your agent?"

"She's a business student with just months to go. She's got my best interest at heart, and—"

"While it lasts," my mother said. "You can't be this naïve, can you? And who knows what kind of issues she'll have with her trust." She made it seem as if Hope was using me to get help with the trust, or that maybe she didn't think there was a trust at all.

"Mom, just hold off on your judgments until you meet her, please." Just then, there were headlights shining through the window. "That's her."

"Oh, I can't wait." My mother walked over to stand near the sofa as I went to the door.

A moment later, Hope got out of her car and hurried up the walk. "I'm sorry if I'm late. I had a bit of trouble with the cash drawer."

"It's okay," I said as my mother cleared her throat behind me. I said a little prayer that my mother, whose colleagues referred to as the Piranha because of the way she chewed up her opposition, would control herself.

"This is my mother, Olivia Tate. Mom, this is Hope Mayhew."

Hope's eyes brightened with her smile as she turned to my mother and greeted her. "Hello, Mrs. Tate. It's so nice to meet you."

"It's nice to meet you too. I didn't realize the hair would really be pink. I assumed that my son had taken artistic liberties."

"No, ma'am. It's all me. That is to say, I have it done regularly. I've gotten kind of attached to it."

"Well, for pink hair, it does complement your beauty."

"Thank you," Hope said, brushing her fingers through it. She absently placed her hand on her tummy as she turned back to me. "Chris loves it."

"And the person wearing it," I said, kissing her cheek.

My mother narrowed her eyes as if something wasn't sitting right, and I wondered if she could sense that we had big news to share.

She walked over and offered Hope a spot to sit down. "I'd normally take business into my office, but since Chris is my son, I thought we'd make it a more informal environment if that's okay with you?"

"It's fine, thank you. I've been wanting to meet you. I hate that I missed you at the art show." She took a seat on the sofa across from where my mother sat, and I joined her.

"Yes, well, I had a client. Speaking of clients, I hear you have a problem with your trust?" My mother was nothing but efficient. She didn't waste any time getting down to business.

"Oh, yes, the trust. It's just that I've always been told that my trust, which pays me five hundred a week, is set to be released when I'm thirty. My father has always dealt with the business end of that, and while I never had any reason to question it, lately I've wondered if there are any other circumstances of the trust that I need to be concerned about."

"Hope's father is a bit of a control freak. He's demanding she return to New York, and he's holding her allowance over her head."

My mother put down her drink and then picked up her phone from the table between us. "What is your allowance? Is it separate from your trust?"

"Yes, it's five hundred more a week more, but that's my father's money. He said I should be able to live on four grand a month. But some of that is given back for rent and insurance on the car. It's quite expensive."

"And does he pay those?" my mother asked, typing into her phone when Hope responded with a nod. "How much is your trust worth? If you don't mind me asking?" She eased back and crossed her legs, typing every bit of information that was said between them.

"The last time I was told, it was five hundred fifty thousand."

My mother's eyes widened. "And you need me to do what exactly?" She raised up and took a sip from her drink.

Hope moved forward in her seat. "I'd like you to look into it. Make sure it's all in working order, find out what the trust is actually worth, and make sure there aren't any special terms, limits, and clauses. I also need to make sure my father isn't able to hold it hostage if I don't do his bidding."

"I can do that," my mother said easily.

"Thank you," Hope responded, breathing a sigh of relief. She put her hand on her stomach again and then held my hand.

"Well, it's really no problem at all. It's a matter of a few phone calls. Do you remember the lawyer's name who handled it?"

"Yes, it's Huntington. Patrick Huntington. He's out of New York."

She narrowed her eyes. "I know Pat Huntington. I tried a case with him in my early days of practice. I'll give him a call." Mom eased back again, this time putting the phone down in her lap. "So, is there another reason you two love-birds wanted to come by tonight?"

"I guess we do have a bit of news," I said, feeling my heart race. I was either about to piss her off or make her a happy woman; I wouldn't know until I told her.

"Well, don't keep me in suspense. I mean, I've already learned that you are trying to get her to represent you. What's next?"

"You told her? I mean, I haven't decided." Hope looked a bit embarrassed.

"Well, I hope you're not already planning a wedding. I mean, it's a bit soon, isn't it?"

Hope turned to look at me. I could see the fear in her eyes. I decided just to rip the band aid off.

"Actually, Mom. It's a lot more exciting than that. We're going to have a baby."

My mother sat stone still for a moment, and just when Hope laid her head on my shoulder, she spoke. "Well, then, ignore that last part. When is the wedding?"

I couldn't believe she was worried about marriage. "That's what you have to say? We're still figuring things out."

"No, I mean... Well, congratulations." She put her hand on her heart. "When is the precious little one due?" It was still hard to tell how my mother felt, and it wasn't until I saw tears in her eyes that I knew everything was going to be okay. She was one happy lady.

And with any luck, she would find something out about the trust and make Hope happy too.

CHAPTER 20

HOPE

Chris's voice woke me, and I could tell that he was upset and downstairs. "Did you call that other client? I wish you'd do what I ask." He grew angrier by the minute, and I wasn't sure who he was talking to. Someone had surely earned the rage.

It had been two days ago that I had met his mother, and I still hadn't told him if I would represent him. I got up and walked to the railing, looking down into the living room where he paced back and forth across the rug.

"It was a lot of money, Virginia, and you just let it slip through your hands. Meanwhile, I need a payday. It's been weeks." He paused a moment, putting his hand on the back of his neck. "I'm still waiting for an answer." He took a few more steps. "She's thinking it over. You'll know soon enough. But you really shouldn't worry about that. You should worry about the museum's commission."

He glanced up at me and then turned his back to me. "I'll call you back." He hung up and tossed his phone into the chair as I made my way down.

"I had no idea you were having so much trouble with the gallery." I wish he would have explained it all to me. We were going to have to learn to communicate better or at least come to an understanding. But he probably didn't want to worry me, which was refreshing. Especially since my father didn't care how stressed out with worry I got.

He looked tired, and I realized the call must have woke him up. "I didn't want to bother you with it, but Virginia is being impossible. She's refusing to sell the art for less than what *she* wants, and she's got one customer interested who she will not call back. I tell you, it's really frustrating."

I hated to see him upset and knew what I needed to do to give him some relief. "Well, I've thought about your offer, and I accept. I'll be your agent."

His shoulders slumped, and he let out a breath of relief. But I wasn't done.

"I know that's what you wanted," I said. "But I'm warning you, the minute it looks like it's going to come between us, I'm going to bow out. I won't let it hurt our relationship. With the baby, it's too important."

He nodded. "I agree, and I completely respect that. I'll call her back in a minute and tell her that you'll be in touch. The sooner you can take over, the better."

He walked over and pulled me into his arms. "I thought we might go apartment hunting later. Maybe look at a house or two?"

"That sounds fun, but a little expensive. Have you talked to your mom yet?"

"She said she's calling you when she finds out more, but she did confide that she thinks there's something shady with the amount you're getting. It's usually more than that, and especially for your age. She said to have a trust go until you're thirty isn't normal."

"I hope she's right, but then it will mean my father has basically been lying to me all of this time, and who knows what's happening to my money?"

"She'll get to the bottom of it. It's what she's good at." He held me close. "Thank you for taking the job. I already can tell a huge weight has been lifted. It is so hard to be creative with this kind of stuff holding over my head. And while I know you won't be responsible for everything, just having someone take care of negotiations is a lifesaver."

"I'm glad to help." I kissed him and then moved a bit closer until my body was pressed against his.

"How do you feel about everything? Are you good?"

"It's all going to work out, isn't it?" I was excited about the days ahead. Even though my father still made me anxious, things had been much better since Chris was in my life for good. I felt protected, as if I had my own defense team building against my father.

But I still wasn't ready to confront him.

"It's all going to be okay. I promise. I have the realtor looking for the perfect place for us, and I've got some money in the bank we can use for a down payment."

"I have some stuffed aside as well." I had started stuffing money away as soon as my father started threatening to cut me off again. He did it every now and then as a scare tactic, but he'd never gotten so close as this.

"I love it when you have the day off," he whispered in my ear. "And this wasn't how I planned our morning, just in case you wondered."

"Oh? You had plans?" I wanted to strangle Virginia for calling and ruining our morning.

"Yes. Big plans." He held his hands wide. "But they're better explained back upstairs in the bedroom. So, we should go on up."

I gave him a look. "In the bedroom or the bed? You're not going to paint me again, are you?" He had two paintings that weren't even finished, and he had already started a third. I was afraid he was going to get sick of me.

"Mm, I just might. You should feel how stiff my brush is."

I let my hand move down between his legs. "That's really stiff," I said, playing along. "I've got a canvas. You can beat it against me if you want."

"Can I be as rough as I want?" He waggled his brows. "I'll make sure not to hurt you."

"I'm fairly certain I won't break." I stroked his cock, and he closed his eyes and moaned. Then he picked me up over his shoulder and carried me up the stairs.

Once upstairs, he made his way to the bed with me and then gently placed me on the edge.

As I made a move to scoot up to the middle, he shook his head. "No, don't move. I've got plans, remember?"

He chuckled, dropping to his knees in front of me. He reached for my waistband and tugged my sleep shorts down. Then he kissed my thighs and moved upward, dragging his tongue against my flesh until he couldn't get any higher. He kissed me there, licking and teasing. Then he grabbed my knees and opened my legs wider to give him better access.

I rolled my hips, enjoying the pleasure that he gave me as I tousled his hair. Then he moved up to kiss me, giving me a taste of my honey from his tongue.

I eased back, lying flat, as he picked up my legs and pulled me toward him. He teased his cock at my slit and then nudged his fat head against it, pushing until he had entered me. He pumped his hips, going a little deeper into my channel with each throbbing thrust.

"I like your plan," I said. "It feels so good."

He smiled that devilish smile of his, and the look on his face was pure smolder as he worked me over.

I came a few seconds later, the feeling overtaking me until I couldn't hold back anymore, not that I wanted to or tried.

"You feel amazing when you come for me." He quickened his pace, moving forward over me as he thrust harder, rutting deep, grinding against me.

"Oh, Chris. That's so good." He teased that spot until I found my release again, and then he pulled me against him, lifting me up into his arms. He fucked me standing, bouncing me on his cock as I held on to his shoulders for dear life. Then he brought me to the bathroom and placed my ass up on the counter.

Whatever plan he had, he abandoned it long enough for a few thrusts, and I cried out as the cold mirror hit my back.

He stepped away, putting his fingers inside, stroking my channel as he rubbed my clit with his thumb. He turned on the shower and then walked back over to kiss me, before dropping to his knees and eating my pussy, his tongue flicking fast across my clit.

Then he stood up and brought me forward, lifting me from the counter. He carried me into the spray and placed me on my feet. "Spin around," he said.

I did exactly what he said, knowing that I was going to enjoy whatever else he had planned for me. I placed my hands against the shower as his fingers explored my body, his mouth planting watery kisses beneath the spray.

He moved behind me, cupping my breasts, pushing them together as he tilted my hips up. I closed my eyes as he teased my ass with his cock. Then he entered my pussy, working up a steady rhythm as he reached around and stroked my clit.

It sent me over the edge, and soon, I was limp as a noodle, my body pressed against the tile. "Don't stop, Chris."

"I'm not, baby. I'm going to make you come for me until you can't stand. Then I'm going to carry you to the bed and fuck you some more."

The words spoken into my ear gave me chills up my back and down the sensitive part of my ass, and when I giggled, he gave a soft laugh against my neck, then slapped my bottom softly. It was just enough to send a lick of heat between my legs, and it made me cry out.

"You're so sexy, letting me take you hard. I can't wait to fill you up."

"Do it," I said. "I want it." I was ready for anything he wanted to give me, and just how I asked, he gave it to me. Hard and deep.

He pulled out and met my eyes before we kissed. Then I dropped down to my knees only to find he was ready to go.

I took him into my mouth, swirling my tongue around where his bulbous, fleshy head met his shaft.

I could taste our scents on him as I took him deep, relaxing my throat and hoping I didn't choke. But as soon as I thought about it, I did, gagging a little. I pulled away with watery eyes, and he lost it, moaning my name as he came on my tongue.

I licked my lips and swallowed it down, twirling my tongue around his head to ensure I got every drop.

"That was amazing," he said. "You look so beautiful like that—the look in your eyes when you are pleasuring me. It's the hottest thing in the world knowing you're that into it." His praise made me feel special, and so did after when he held me close and kissed my shoulder. We stood there, under the warm spray, caressing each other's bodies and relaxing.

"Let's get out of here," he said. "I'll get us some breakfast, and we can come back later for round three. How about pancakes? I make a mean blueberry."

"Sounds good to me." I was up for anything he wanted and loved that I made him happy.

As if he read my mind, he nuzzled against me. "You make me happy, Hope." He brushed my wet hair from my face. "I can't remember the last time I felt like everything was perfect. And you and that baby, you're everything to me."

"Likewise," she said with a quiet voice. "I don't ever want to lose you."

"You won't, baby. I promise. We're going to make it all work out. Together, we're an unstoppable force. You'll see."

I sure hoped he was right.

Since I didn't have anything to do while Hope was at work, I prepared for our afternoon meeting with Virginia by picking up Hope's business cards from the print shop and organizing her proposals based on what I had in stock. I wanted more space, at least until the wall-sized work was sold.

Having Hope as my agent was going to work out for us both.

When her shift was over, I drove over to Paddy's and picked her up, and she changed in the car, wanting to make a better impression. "Did you bring my shoes?" she asked, pulling on her shirt.

"They're in the back," I said, trying to keep my eyes on the road. It was hard, seeing as she was sitting in the front seat with her ass hanging out.

She undid her seat belt and then reached over the seat. "Thanks. I didn't want to meet her in my scrubby work clothes. It's bad enough she probably hates me already."

"She should be glad I hired you. It's been a nightmare every single time a sale comes up."

"Speaking of nightmares, any word from your mother about my trust?"

"Not yet, but she said that the lawyer was trying to play hardball. She thinks it's because your father is pulling strings. He's probably been influencing the man the whole time."

"Well, as long as she has my permission, there shouldn't be any trouble."

Hope was a bit naïve at just how far her father was willing to go, and I didn't want to tell her that I thought we'd find out there was more to it. I just hoped that he hadn't completely screwed his daughter out of her trust. Why else was he so hell-bent on being in charge?

"In theory, there shouldn't be any problems, but this is your father we're talking about."

"Right." She let out a long sigh. "I don't know why he has to be so awful. He texted me a photo of Aunt Mary's retirement cake and then one of her empty chair from her old office that he expects me to take over. He said it needed a warm body to fill it for a change. He's always hated his sister. He's never going to let me be happy." She put her hands around her middle.

"You need to stop dwelling on him. You spend too many hours a day worrying about him. Why do you even care at this point?"

"Because he's the only family I have left. The only parent. Maybe deep down inside, I just want him to love me."

"I'm sure he does. He just doesn't know how to show it." I wanted to ask if she'd considered letting me meet the man. I had a feeling once he wasn't the only man in her life, his tune would change, but Hope was not as convinced, and I was trying to get her to forget him for the moment. I never knew what to expect when she was holding her stomach. Was it because of the baby? Or because she was stressing out again?

I had to wonder if her father would warm up to the baby in a different way. If my mother was any indication, we might be surprised by the reaction.

Finally, she was finished getting dressed, and she pulled down the mirror in front of her and looked at her hair and makeup.

"What if I change my hair? Will you still love me and want to paint me?"

"I don't love you for your hair, and if you want to do that, then I'll support your decision. I can still paint you with any color hair and want to."

"Your mother doesn't like my hair," she said, putting the mirror up. She eased back in her seat as I pulled into the art gallery.

"You shouldn't worry about what she thinks."

"But I'm going to be a mother. And I only did it to piss off my father. Although I have to admit, I love it."

"So, what? Keep it. It's really up to you." I didn't really want her to change her hair, but it was ultimately her decision.

"I don't know." She ran her hand through it. "I guess we'll wait and see."

I parked the car and then walked around to get her door. She got out, and I took her hand. We walked inside the gallery a united front. While I expected Virginia to have an attitude, she met us upfront with a grin.

"Christian," she said, coming over to greet me with the usual hug and a kiss on each cheek. She turned to see Hope, and while her expression had faded a bit, it seemed to mostly be from worry. "How are you, darling?"

"I'm just fine, thank you. I'd like for us to sit down and talk if at all possible?"

"Sure," Virginia said. "Come back here to my office." She led us down the hall and around the corner, and then she opened her door and offered us a seat. "Make yourself at home."

"Thank you," Hope said. "I was told that you had talked to a potential client and he was interested in the painting?"

"Oh, yes, but I've actually misplaced the number. I'm so sorry."

Hope glanced at me, my anger building.

"Are you kidding me?" I asked. "I thought you said you had it?"

"I thought I did as well, but the cleaning lady must have tossed it. I had put it aside in case the other deal fell through."

"Why not let them bid it out?" Hope asked. "You could have not only gotten a sale, but you could have doubled your profit. You killed the possibility when you decided to only work with one client."

"I thought for sure that they were going to buy it. I mean, they had all but pulled the trigger."

"I heard about that. They were so close until what? Is that when you countered without asking Chris?"

"I have made many negotiations for Christian in the past, and I don't see how this time should be any different."

I couldn't just sit there and let her act as if she'd acted with my best interest at heart. "You can't refuse a perfectly decent offer just because you wanted a bigger commission. And I might add that I find it strangely suspicious that you 'lost' that other lead, especially now that Hope is taking over."

"Are you insinuating that I lost the lead on purpose?" She leaned forward. "Well, don't you have a big pair. I would never do anything like that."

"Well, I should hope not, but at least I won't have to worry about it anymore." I took Hope's business cards from my pocket and left them on the table. "Here. These are for anyone interested in my work going forward. We'll take it from here."

"And I'd like to negotiate more space for Chris," Hope continued. "He has many other works, and while we appreciate the back wall, he's looking to expand a bit. I see that you have other areas with more space. Perhaps we could work out an arrangement?"

It was in Virginia's best interest to play along. I had been one of her most valuable artists for the past two years. "Okay, I'm sure we can arrange something. But I want more than one item. No more groupings."

"That's fair."

Virginia took a pad and paper and scribbled on it. "Here are my terms, and this is the best proposal I have for him right now. If something changes, then we'll see where we're at."

Hope took the paper and shook her head. "I think something like this—" She picked up the pen and scribbled in her own amount. "—and we won't give you a penny more. Take it or leave it."

The way she looked Virginia in the eyes, demanding what I'd get, really turned me on.

Virginia took the paper and hesitated a moment before glancing at me. "I can make this work. But I want at least eight works here by the first of September. And she has to be the model in at least half. There is a call for those. I think they'll do well."

Hope held out her hand. "You've got a deal."

Not only had we negotiated for more space, but I was all set to make way more money. I was glad that she had played hardball for me.

As we rose up, I couldn't help but kiss her.

Virginia paled. "Well, I guess that's why you drove such a hard bargain. You're playing every pocket."

"I beg your pardon?" I asked. "That was way out of line."

"I've known you a long time, Christian. You should know I would never say anything to hurt you. But you'll have to excuse me for not being happy about this arrangement."

"You have no idea what kind of arrangement we have. We're in love, and we're having a baby."

Her face paled even more, this time taking on a sickly green expression. "Oh, I'm so sorry, Christian."

"It's Chris. And you should be sorry. She's good for me. She has my best interest at heart, unlike you. You've been out for your own gain since I started showing here. It's obvious. But I have a family now, and I'm not going to let you keep taking advantage. So, this isn't a con job. It's a family affair. You should learn the difference before you go running off at the mouth."

I was livid, and maybe I had been a little harsh on the woman, but damn. She needed to learn to mind her business and do her job.

"Forgive me. And congratulations. I'll expect those paintings by September first." With that, she got up and showed us to the door, and I had to admit, I felt a little bad for being so hard.

"Well, that went a little crazy," Hope said when we got into the car.

"I'm sorry. I should have just let you work the deal, but she's the one who keeps making it personal. She feels like since she came to me my senior year that she owns me. I'm the one who's done the painting and made the money. I don't owe her everything. And I'm not going to let someone sit there and bad-mouth you. She had no right to make assumptions over hurt feelings."

"Do you think she really lost the information?"

"I don't know. But if she had it in mind to give it to us, she isn't now." I wouldn't if I was her. And I needed to let things settle down a bit and try to repair the relationship. If she couldn't, then that was on her.

Hope gave me a reassuring look. "There will be more interest. We left the cards, and you have the site updated, right?"

"I did that earlier. I'm ready."

"So, now that's done, what's next on the agenda?" She waggled her brows at me. "Did you know that my hormones are so whacked out that I stay horny all the damn time now?" She batted her lashes at me and then moved a little closer, blowing in my ear.

"Oh yeah?" I asked, giving her the side-eye.

"Mhm." She ran her hand up my leg, stroking my thigh and the big bulge in my pants. "And you really turned me on back there."

"Yeah? Well, you turn me on too, in case you can't tell."

"Mm." She licked her lips. "Maybe I should help you with that." She moved toward my lap, and I eased the seat back and drove across town to where the streets had less traffic, taking the long way home.

I couldn't wait to get her to bed.

As I walked from class, waiting on Chris to call, my phone rang. I hurried to pick it up, not bothering to look at the caller ID. "Hey, sexy," I said, using my sultriest, seductive tone.

"Excuse me?" my father said, causing my stomach to roll and a mortifying expression to be displayed on my face. "Who the hell did you think this is?"

"I'm so sorry, Dad." I wondered why he was calling.

"I'm in town, and I want to see you."

"I can't see you tonight, Dad, I have to work."

"You're always working. Aren't I paying for everything? Have you got a shopping addiction or something?"

"No, I got a job because you keep threatening to *stop* paying for everything."

"Well, I guess that's also why you've been nosing around in my business."

My back stiffened. I knew that he was talking about the trust, but I had to play stupid. "What do you mean your business?" If anything, the trust was my business.

"Don't play stupid with me, Hope. I know you've got some Chicago lawyer digging around in my affairs. You should know by now that you're not going to get away with something like that without me finding out. I have eyes and ears everywhere. And just what are you hoping to gain? I demand that you tell that bitch to mind her own business. Do you hear me?"

I was fuming. "The trust is mine. I can check on anything I want."

"I have things in place to protect you. You need to leave well enough alone."

"Why? Because you don't want me to find out that you've been duping me all this time?"

"You watch it, young lady. I'm your father, and I will have respect from you. Do you understand?"

I held my belly, the ulcer in there feeling like I was being jabbed with a red-hot poker. "I have questions and I deserve answers."

"Well, then you can ask me. I'll see you while I'm in town, and we'll get to the bottom of this. As for whoever you're whoring around with, I suggest you break it off. And if I find out it's that broke-ass artist, you're going to be sorry."

"Don't talk about Chris that way." It came out before I could stop myself. "He's a good man. You don't know anything about him."

"So, you are seeing him? You think I don't know what a guy like that wants with you? He wants your money, Hope. He wants your trust. That's all that type is good for."

"I have to get to work," I said, holding my hand on my belly. I felt a wave of nausea roll across me, and then I walked over to the nearest tree and tried to get my balance.

"I expect to see you tomorrow, Hope. We have a lot to

talk about. And just in case you try to no-show me, I think you should know that I'm not leaving this fucking town until you come and see me. As a matter of fact, I'll be at your place bright and early. I expect you to be there."

Just when I heard the phone go dead, I heard my name. "Hope!"

Nicole came running over to me. "Are you okay?"

I spun around to find her standing with Puck, who was walking her to class. She had told me that they were supposed to have a dinner date, but I hadn't expected to see him at the university.

"That was my dad. He's in town. I'm a little sick. I felt like I was losing my balance."

"Whoa, little mama. Maybe I should take you home." Puck held out his hand to steady me. "You look a little woozy."

"I have to go to work," I said, trying to stand up straight and fight the feeling of nausea.

"What did he say?" Nicole asked.

"He knows about the investigation into the trust, and he's pissed. He also knows I'm still seeing Chris. And he said that I have to see him tomorrow. I don't think I can." It happened faster than I thought, and I began to be sick behind the tree. The acid burned coming up.

Puck rubbed my back. "Chris isn't going to like this. I know you have to work, but I really think I should call him."

I wiped my mouth, stepping away from the tree. "No, don't bother him. He's painting, and he's got so much to do." He had his painting to worry about, and this problem would be there come the next morning. I would deal with it then. Alone.

Puck and Nicole exchanged a look. "Will you at least

drive her to work?" Nicole asked. She stressed the words, and I almost felt like they were up to something.

"Yeah, I can't let her drive like this," he said. I must have been visibly shaking. I know I was inside. "I still think you should call into work. Maybe just see what Chris thinks?"

I didn't want him to freak out and search the city for my father so he could beat his ass. Although, seeing my father get his comeuppance would be a treat if it wouldn't lead to his own retaliation.

"I'll let you drive me to work. I'll be fine. I just need to calm down." I felt like such an idiot with everyone doting over me. I wasn't a child. I had to put the stress aside for the baby and head to work. I had money to make in case my father cut me off after this. He had never been so angry, so full of hate. I'd just have to deal with my dad the next day and hope that Chris didn't learn how bad the phone call was. I didn't need for things to get any worse.

"Come on," Puck said. "It's against my better judgment, but I'll do it."

"You're the best," Nicole said. "Thanks." She kissed him on the lips, and he flashed her a wink before taking me by the hand. "Come on," he said. "Hold on to old Puck. If you fall, I'm sure Chris is going to kill me, so don't okay?"

"Thanks for doing this."

"It's cool. No worries. Just don't let Chris cut my balls off while I sleep. He's really crazy when it comes to you and that baby."

Puck drove me to work, and when I got there, I got out of the car to find Chris standing at the entrance.

"You called him anyway?" I couldn't believe it. When had he had the time?

"Not me," he said, holding up his hands from the wheel.

Chris walked out to join us. "Nicole called me. She was

worried about you and rightly so—you're so pale you look like you've seen a ghost."

"It's from riding with Puck. He drives like a madman."

"That's my cue; she's all yours." Puck revved the engine, and when I stepped away, he drove off.

"I can't believe she ratted me out."

"She cares about you. What I can't believe is that you came to work."

"Jesus. I'm not an invalid and I don't need to be treated like a porcelain doll. I felt a little woozy. It happens. I'm pregnant. It's all part of the deal. I have a job to do."

"And you have enough time that you can afford a day off without losing that job."

I started to the door. "I can't just take a day off every time I feel queasy. I'd never go in."

Chris grabbed my shoulder. "You're not going in. I've already talked to Jude. She wants you to go home and lie down."

His voice was so stern, I could tell that he was pissed off at me. I began to cry, not because he was angry but because I was. Everyone in my life was trying to control me and I'd had enough.

"Stop it," he said. "You're not doing any good crying."

"I've had enough of everyone else telling me how to live my life."

"Baby, I'm not trying to tell you how to live your life. I'm scared that you're not taking care of yourself. And quite honestly, I don't know what your old man said, but I want to punch him in the face, which I know won't do you any good. So we're going home."

"He's in the city. He wants to see me tomorrow. I'll have to go and stay in the apartment alone. In case he shows up."

"No, you're not. You're staying with me, and tomorrow, we're both going over there. Together."

"That's only going to add to my stress, Chris. He's not going to hurt me."

"He's already doing that, dammit." He took my hand and led me to the car, and then, after helping me into my seat, he slammed the door and walked around to get in with me. "You need to rest. I'll take you home later, but work is done, and you're not going home alone right now."

"I'm sorry," I said after a beat. "I should have called you."

"Yeah, I had to hear everything from Nicole. She's a good friend, you know? She cares about you."

"She told you everything?"

"She told me enough. You can wait until you're settled down, and we'll calmly talk it out. But for now, just lay the seat back and close your eyes."

I did as he told me, knowing if I didn't, he would only keep chirping. When we got back to his building, Puck was standing in at the door.

"Thanks again, Puck."

"Anytime, Hope." He turned and went to his station as we walked through the tattoo parlor to the stairs.

Chris remained quiet, and I wondered if that was because he was angry, or because he was worried.

When we took to the stairs, he put his arm around me, and then we walked up together. "I can carry you if you want," he said after a couple of slow steps.

"No, I'm fine. I'm just taking my time."

We finally got inside the apartment, and he closed and locked the door. "Do you want to walk up the stairs or stay down here?"

"Could we just stay here a little while?"

"Yeah, anything you want." He waited for me to sit down and then walked to the kitchen. "Do you want anything to eat?"

"I'm not hungry."

"You need to eat."

"Fine. I'll have some crackers," I said, knowing not to argue. He was just going to keep on until I had something in my stomach.

He brought over a sleeve of crackers, a butter knife, and the jar of peanut butter, even though I hadn't asked for it. And then he sat down beside me and ate a few. Finally, I joined him, both of us quiet until we ran out of crackers.

"He said that it's going to get ugly if you show up. I don't want you to have to deal with him."

"Stop. Let's worry about it tomorrow, okay?"

"Fine." I was just going to stress about it anyway.

We curled up on the couch for some TV, and at dinnertime, he ordered something from the Grind that would be easy on my stomach as we watched a movie.

Nicole called to check to check on me, making sure to keep me calm. I just wasn't sure what was going to happen when the sun came up.

CHAPTER 23

CHRIS

Hope lay on the couch with her head in my lap as we watched the movie, and before I knew it, she was dozing off. I let her stay that way for nearly an hour before she stirred.

"Do you want to go upstairs, baby?"

"Let's just stay here a minute." She sat up and glanced at the TV. "What happened to the movie?"

"It ended about half an hour ago. You fell asleep."

"Ugh. It's just so frustrating. I feel like I'm not in control of my body anymore."

"You are, Hope. You just had a little too much excitement today."

"He expects to see me in the morning. I should really go home."

"He knows that we're together now, right?"

"Yeah. And he's not happy." She closed her eyes as her expression changed. Her cheeks reddened. "It didn't help that I answered the phone with a 'hello sexy' when he called."

"You didn't," I said, trying hard not to laugh.

She nodded as she covered her face with both hands. "Oh yeah, I did. I thought it was you. And that set him off. He said if you're there, things will get ugly. He is liable to try and make me go back home. And I know it's going to be war when I refuse. When he hears I'm pregnant, he's going to disown me."

"You don't think the baby could soften his black heart a tiny bit?"

"I'm not sure I want him to ever know about the baby."

"He has to know. It's going to come out eventually, Hope. Keeping things from him hasn't helped. So, I think we both need to go and see him and tell him what's going on."

"No, Chris. Please let me do this alone. I know my father. If I just show up and deal with him, he's going to go back to New York, and I can go on with my life." She didn't want to stand up to him, which was only going to make him worse.

"I'm not letting you go alone. Besides, it's the only way this is going to work for me. I'm not living in secret from your father. I'm a man; I'm going to go and stand up for you, and for us. I'm not afraid of him."

About that time, the phone rang. "It's my mother. It could be about the trust." I answered and eased back against the cushion. Hope slid closer, so I put my arm around her. "Hey, Mom. Is everything all right?" She usually didn't call me after eight.

"Yes, and no," she said. "I just finished an amazing dinner, and I have some news for you and Hope."

"About the trust?" It couldn't be anything else, but I wanted Hope to know the conversation took a turn in her direction. "Could I put you on speakerphone?"

"Yes, I'd like you both to hear it."

I put the phone on speaker and Hope cuddled closer. "Did you talk to Patrick Huntington?" she asked my mother.

"Yes. He tried to make it hard at first, but then I pointed out that you had rights and enough money to sue him. So, after some attempts, I got the copy of your trust sent to me. And I learned something that you're not going to like."

I stroked Hope's back, hoping she wasn't going to be sick again. "I don't like the sound of that. Hope has already had a hard day because of that man. What's next?"

"Hope, I'm sorry to tell you this, but your father has been skimming off of your trust."

"He's stealing from me?"

"It looks like it, but that's what I wanted to talk to you about."

I was so livid I could feel my anger boiling. The only thing keeping me together was that Hope needed me to keep my cool. But inside, I wanted to beat her father to a bloody pulp. "I'm not sure why there's a problem. He either is, or he isn't."

"Hope, you said that you get five hundred a week. And that your father gives you money from his own pocket for an allowance?"

"Yes, for rent and other expenses. It's the only way I can make it."

"I see. And that amount is?"

"An extra five. It's usually around four grand a month, but I never see that much with my rent. He insists I live where I do for the security, but the rent is expensive, and he takes some back for insurance on the car."

"Hope, all he's doing is giving you five hundred of your

own money, while he pockets half. And he's still making you pay expenses."

"Wait," I said, adding it all up in my head. "You're saying she should be getting two grand a week?"

"Yes, from the time she turned eighteen, and with her attending college, she should be getting two grand a week. He's keeping half for himself."

Hope sat up straight. "Are you kidding? He's been holding my own money over my head all of this time?

"Honey, you might want to brace yourself, because there's more."

"You mean it gets worse?"

"Well, that is a matter of perspective, but it certainly gets more interesting," she said.

I hugged Hope tight. "Just tell her." I had a feeling it was going to be so devastating that she was going to need some extra comfort and support.

"You said your trust was worth around five hundred thousand?"

"Something like that." She sagged in my arms. "How much has he stolen?"

"I'm not sure about that, but your trust isn't five hundred grand. It's over nine hundred thousand dollars, Hope. And growing."

"You mean when I'm thirty, I'll have over a million dollars?" Her jaw dropped, and she blinked several times. But before she could say another word, my mother had more to tell her.

"Hope, honey. You're not getting the trust at thirty. It seems your father was just telling you that so he could have more time to skim from it. You should get your trust at twenty-five."

"But that's just months away. I turn twenty-five in October."

"That's why he's been ragging on you so hard lately to get you to come to the company, where he has a tighter hold on you and the money. He knows you're finishing college soon, and he won't be able to use your tuition as part of your leverage. He's trying to keep you close and your money closer. It has to be."

"How could he do that?"

"I'm not sure, honey, but I've already taken the proper legal actions on your behalf. You'll have to name a new attorney to look over your trust, but I'd encourage you to not use anyone your father recommends. It seems Patrick Huntington was in pretty deep."

"Can I sue him?"

"Oh yeah," my mother said. "Huntington and your father. But I'd figure out where that money he's been taking is going. If he's put it into property, or a business, you could take possession of it."

"Do you have any way of checking into that?"

"I could form a team to look into it if you want?"

Hope thought a minute. "I guess I can afford it," she said, squeezing my hand. "I want to make him pay. He owes me for all the misery he's caused."

My mother made a sound of agreement. "I'll get right on it," she said. "First thing in the morning, I'll be filing against both of them."

"Can you find someone who can handle my trust? Someone local?"

"I will give you a few names. It's best that you make that decision, Hope. You're going to have to be more accountable for your income, but you can do it."

She looked into my eyes. "Thank you for everything, Ms. Tate."

"Call me, Olivia, dear. And don't let that man upset you anymore. He might be your father, but no one who treats you badly is worth it. And you need to protect my grand-baby too."

After we ended the call, I pulled her into my arms and hugged her. "There's no way I'm not going with you tomorrow."

"I want you there. I'm going to take back my life and my money, and I'm going to tell him just what I think of him, right after I find out what he's been doing with my money."

"Just make sure to keep calm, Hope. I don't want you getting all keyed up over this. He's not worth risking your health and the health of our baby."

"Don't worry. For probably the first time, I'm not scared of him anymore. I'm angry. Angry that I've put up with this for so long, and angry that he's made me sick. He doesn't even care about me. And I've let him rule over me, holding his money over my head when it was rightfully mine all along. My mother left me that trust, and I'm going to fight him tooth and nail until I get every dime back."

She was getting pretty excited, but this was a new strength I'd never seen from her before. She was so beau-tiful in that moment that I itched to paint her, to capture the moment forever. I wanted to snap a photo, but I decided to let it burn into my memory instead. I'd save it for later. This was her moment, and I had a feeling it hadn't all sank in.

"Well, your life is really about to change," I said. It was nice knowing that she wouldn't have a care in the world, and I couldn't ask for a bigger blessing for my child.

"*Our* lives. We're going to be able to have whatever we

need and want. No more worrying about finances and how I'm going to make it. I can breathe. I can quit Paddy's."

"You could *buy* Paddy's," I said with a laugh. I was trying to lighten the mood since hers seemed to be all over the place.

Hope began to chuckle. "I could!" She took a deep breath and let it out. "Too bad money can't solve every problem." I could tell she was disappointed. "I feel like I lost my dad today." Her face fell. "All I ever wanted from him was for him to love me. I guess he never has. He sure didn't care about my mother. In fact, all he's ever really loved was money."

"You should tell him that's how you feel. I'm sure he'll tell you it's not true." I couldn't imagine my child ever thinking that I didn't love them. And how could anyone not love Hope? She was amazing. He was lucky to be so blessed.

She didn't look convinced. "I'm not sure. I mean, I don't know if it even matters. All I know is, come tomorrow, I'm giving him a piece of my mind, once and for all."

"Of course it matters. And how he treats you matters." I had a lot I wanted to say to her old man, and I was sure that saying it all on the first day we met wasn't a good idea, but I also knew I'd have a long time—the rest of our lives, for the opportunity to arise. Knowing her father, it wouldn't be the final showdown.

CHAPTER 24

HOPE

Early the next morning, Chris had taken me home. And after a long, hot shower and spending half an hour on my hair, I was nearly ready to go and meet with my father.

"Hope, are you sure you're feeling better?" Chris asked while I went to my closet to find my shoes.

"I'm good," I said as the butterflies in my stomach swung their tiny swords. I had psyched myself up all night over this meeting, and I was ready to get it over with. "He was angry when I called earlier to tell him that I'd have to meet him a little later, but he'll get over it."

"Or he won't," Chris said with a shrug. "Either way, we're not letting him interfere with our lives." He walked up behind me and zipped up my dress.

I turned to face him, giving him a pleading look. "Just promise me that you won't start a fight with him. I don't want you to get arrested for battering an old man." Things were bad enough as they were.

"I promise. I'm going to keep my fists to myself. But my

words? I can't promise you anything. If he upsets you, all bets are off."

I took a deep breath and then released it, hoping it would keep me calm. "Are *you* ready?"

"Oh, yeah," he said. "I've been ready. Let's get this behind us so we can move forward."

I wanted to move forward more than anything, and I hated that things were this way. It was not only upsetting but embarrassing. I was lucky to have someone like Chris, who was willing to stick it out with me.

"I'm ready to go house hunting," I said, trying to look forward to happier things as I grabbed my handbag. "Did you talk to Puck? Does he want to rent the apartment?"

Chris walked to the door. "Yeah, he is, actually. And he said he wanted to buy the couch. I think he's grown rather attached to it."

The idea of Puck saying that made me giggle. "He's a strange one."

"He's infatuated with Nicole. I hope she's ready for him."

We left my apartment making small talk about our friends, and we somehow managed to keep the same topic all the way to the restaurant, where, when we arrived twenty minutes later, we found my father sitting at the table with a frustrated look on his face.

When I approached, he looked up. He didn't even have a smile for me. Instead, his face was a blank mask until he spotted Chris behind me.

Then his mouth turned into a tight line, his jaw tensed.

"Hello, Dad. This is my boyfriend, Chris. Chris, this is my father, Kenneth Mayhew."

My father, who regarded him with a curt nod, got to his

feet as Chris pulled out a chair and then waited until I sat to be seated.

"Chris. I would say it's good to meet you, but I'm not sure what it is that you're doing here. I was supposed to be meeting with my daughter. We had personal business to discuss."

Chris sat beside me. "That's actually *why* I'm here. I'm part of her personal business."

My father sat up straight in his chair as if to posture over him. "Well then, dear, I guess that what I have to say will just have to wait. Perhaps I'll drop by your place later tonight."

"Anything you have to say to me, you can say in front of Chris."

"I hardly think that your finances are any business of his."

"Oh? You mean how you've been dipping into my money all these years?"

His face paled. "I beg your pardon?"

"I'd just like to know one thing, Dad. What did you do with my money? What was worth betraying me? You have the family business; you have your own money, do you not? So why skim from mine?"

He reached for his drink, taking a long pull from the glass before slamming it down. "You don't know what you're talking about."

"Actually, I do, Dad. You see, I had someone look into it. You've been giving me a fourth of my money, pocketing half and holding the other fourth of it over my head. So what did you do with it?"

"Let's not start lecturing me on what I've done. I've helped pay your way is what I've been doing."

"With *my* money. Not yours. So you can stop trying to

lord it over me. And just so you know, as we speak, I'm filing charges against you and your crooked attorney. I'm sure he got a nice chunk of hush money from you."

Something I never thought I'd see happen started to unfold right in front of me. My father started to panic.

"I had to save the company. Why do you think Mary retired early? She needed out before the whole thing went down."

I was shocked. "So you wanted me to give up my life for a failing business? Thanks for looking out for my future," I snapped sarcastically.

"I saved you is what I did. If you didn't have me, you would have wasted that money. You would have spent it frivolously on handbags and shoes, just like your mother always did!"

"You don't know me at all, do you? I got a job to try and pay my own way, and I've never questioned you once about my trust or the money you pay me. I trusted you. I thought you loved me. That you wouldn't do your own flesh and blood that way. But those days are over. I'm done letting you and your people control my money or my life."

"I need that money to keep the business alive, Hope. Don't you see? It's our entire family at risk. Your grandparents' legacy. You owe them that much."

"I don't owe them anything. I have my own life to live. And if the company has been using my money to bail itself out, then I want the controlling interest."

"You can't do that. It's my company. I run it."

"Well, we'll just have to see about that." I could tell my father was getting angrier by the second. But I would not stand down. Not now.

He slammed his hand down on the table, shaking the

plates and silver, the glasses. "How dare you!" he said with a growl of anger in his voice.

"That's enough," Chris spoke up. "Anything you have to say to her, you can do it calmly and rationally, or we will get up and leave."

"Who do you think you are? You're nothing but a low-life, leeching artist. You probably couldn't support yourself, so you decided to con my daughter."

"The only con here is you," she snapped at her father. "We're in love, and we're going to be together."

"Well, how convenient for him," he said with enough acid in his voice to dissolve an elephant. "I'll bet he's got something to do with this little investigation of yours."

"I'm right here. You don't have to address her. You can feel free to address me."

"She's my daughter, my blood, and you're nothing. Don't tell me what I can and can't say to my daughter." He slammed his fist down again, and this time, people began to stare.

I nearly jumped out of my skin, the startle causing me to tense so that my stomach began to hurt even more.

"That's quite enough," Chris fumed. "Can't you see that you upset her? That you make her sick? She's all done being your punching bag. You better get your affairs in order, old man. You're finally going to pay for what you've done to her."

"You have no place here," my father said, trying desperately to hold onto control if the situation.

The words hurt and angered me. I slammed my own fist down, shaking the table. "He has more business here than you do," I said. "He's the fa—"

The cramp hit me so suddenly, it nearly brought me to the floor.

I reached for Chris's arm and gave it a squeeze. He moved quickly, turning in his chair to comfort me. "Are you okay? Is it your ulcer?"

"No. I think it's the baby." I gripped his arm again, feeling an intense pain shoot through my lower abdomen.

"What did you say?" My father went wide-eyed, and I realized that I'd just dropped the bomb without realizing it.

"You heard her," Chris said. "She's pregnant, and you're not doing anything but causing her more grief. She's had an ulcer for months because of you and your threats. But that's all done now. You're through!"

He got to his feet.

Dad got up from his own chair. "Come on, Hope. Let's get you to the doctor."

"I'm not leaving with you," I said as Chris pulled me close.

"We're going to the hospital, and you had better pray she's okay, or I'm coming after you." Chris walked me to the front, threw down some money, and then walked me to the car.

My father followed us out. "Hold up! I'm coming with you."

"Not in my car, you're not. I'm sure you'll manage." He put me in the car, and then as my father hurried to get a cab, Chris drove me to the hospital emergency room.

When we got there, we went inside, Chris carrying me the entire way. Thankfully, they got me right back and put me in a room.

Chris stood by my bed and stroked my hair. "Are you feeling any better?

I shook my head, tears rolling down my face. I was scared that something was really wrong with the baby.

In the hallway, I could hear my father yelling at the

staff. "She's my daughter! I'll go back if I want to!"

I looked up at Chris. "Don't let him come back here," I begged. "I don't want to see him."

A heavyset nurse walked in about that time. "Is he your father?"

"Yes, but please keep him away."

"Oh, don't worry about him, honey. There are four big and scary guards on him as we speak. Now, let me get your vitals."

She came at me with the thermometer, and a moment later, she clipped the blood pressure tester onto my finger.

"Just calm down, baby. He's not coming in here. I won't let him."

"He's so awful," I said with tears in my eyes. The whole ordeal had been terrible and embarrassing.

"Let it out, girl. It's okay if you cry. It's healthy." The machine beeped. "And it might do you some good to relax with your blood pressure so high."

"Is that going to hurt the baby?" We had told her that we were afraid she was having a miscarriage when we rushed past the front desk.

"You need to calm down, honey. You'll be okay. But you need to think about that little one. No matter how small, that baby can sense when you're in distress."

Chris kissed my hand. "It's all going to be okay, Hope."

"You two sit tight a minute, and I'll go see if I can hurry the doctor along."

"I haven't gone to my first visit yet," I told her. I felt it was something she needed to know.

"Okay, I'll have the doctor examine you, then. We're going to make sure everything is okay." She walked out, and I turned my head toward Chris. He came in close to kiss my cheek and stayed there nestled beside me.

"What if something happened to the baby? It's so little still. I don't want to lose it."

"We're not going to lose it."

The doctor came in shortly after, and he did a pelvic exam and an ultrasound. Once I heard that little heartbeat, I knew I loved that little being more than anything in the world.

When the doctor was done, he pulled up a stool and talked to us. "Okay, I've got some good news. The baby is okay. You're still really early in the pregnancy, and your body is working overtime to create that little one. Stress is going to cause a lot of issues. So, if there is any way you can limit stress, I'd suggest it. I'd like to keep you here overnight just to make sure that the bleeding doesn't get any worse, and you were a little dehydrated as well."

I closed my eyes. "There was bleeding?"

"Yes, some. You were spotting a bit when I examined you. Sometimes, the examination makes it a little worse, so we just need to watch that."

Chris and I exchanged a look. "So, what does that mean? Is she still in any danger of miscarrying?"

"I don't think so, but that's not to say the next time she gets stressed, something can't happen. These things are often unpredictable at this stage. So, you need to make sure you keep her as calm as possible. I'll be back in the morning, and if you're all good, I'll send you home."

The doctor finished up, asked us if we had any questions, and then left.

Chris stayed with me a while longer until the nurse came and took me to my room. Then he kissed me and told me he'd be right back. I didn't bother asking. I knew exactly where he was going.

CHAPTER 25

CHRIS

I didn't have to go far to find her father, who was pouting in the waiting room and still arguing with the security guard. "I just want to make sure my daughter is okay. I don't see why I can't go back there."

The guard wasn't putting up with him. "You can sit right there, and when there is information available, someone will provide it."

When her father saw me standing there, he got to his feet. "This is her friend," he said. "Could you give us a moment?"

"Yes," I said. "I'd like a moment to talk privately." I practically stared through him, and I could tell he was a bit uneasy.

The guard walked away, looking back over his shoulder with a warning glare. "I'll be just down the hall."

Mr. Mayhew curled his lip at the man, and then he turned to me and tried to stand up a bit taller.

But he wasn't taller than me. I glared down my nose at

him. "I thought you might want to know what is going on with your daughter and the baby."

His nostrils flared. "Is she okay?"

"They *both* are. Thanks for caring."

"I do care very much. She's all I've got."

"You sure as hell don't treat her that way."

"You wouldn't understand what it's like to have a daughter who doesn't listen. She's always been a bit rebellious and—"

Was this guy for real? "Stop," I said. I couldn't just let him stand there and blame Hope for everything. "None of that is an excuse to steal from her."

He gave me a smug look. "Are you worried there won't be any money left for you? Is that why you care?"

"I care because what you're doing is wrong. And it's hurting the woman I love."

"Oh, sure. I heard you're an artist. Well, her mother was an artist when I met her. She wasted half of her life on that dream, and then the other half on pills and alcohol."

He was making it about himself. "Do you even care that you stress her out so much that you've given her an ulcer?"

Her father shot me a look as if I was being overdramatic. "I'm sure it's not that bad. She has a tendency to let things overwhelm her. She always has. She gets it from her mother and look where that got her." He seemed bitter about her mother's death. Angry that she'd died and left him all alone with a daughter to raise. Maybe that was part of the problem all along.

"It's not an exaggeration. I've seen the way she gets sick just getting a text from you. All of the threats you've given her, wanting her to move home, take the job you want her to have. Every single thing you say to her has made it worse."

He rolled his eyes.

I wanted to tell him to look around. Did he not see that we were standing in the middle of a fucking hospital? It took all I had in me not to go there. "She is strong, except when it comes to you. You're supposed to be strong *for* her, not constantly bringing her down. Instead, you've taken her money and threatened her to the point of her working a job she didn't even need."

"She did that to get under my skin. Just like that pink hair. It makes her look like an idiot. She used to have this long, gorgeous brown hair like her mother. She cut it off because she knew I liked it. Just to spite me. The same reason she started dating you, I'd imagine. I told her to stay away from your kind. Lazy, not the kind of man who wants a real job. Well, now look what a mess you've gotten her into."

"You don't know anything about me, and you damned sure don't know anything about *us*. You've been blathering on so much, you haven't even asked what's wrong with her."

"Well, why don't you go ahead and tell me, since they let you in and not me." He was still pouting like a child being bullied in the schoolyard.

"She's had some bleeding and is a bit dehydrated. They're keeping her overnight. Any more stress and she could lose your grandchild. Is that what you want?"

He glowered at me. "Of course not. And for information, I do care. I *love* my daughter. And while I might have made some mistakes, I only took the money to save her future, not wreck it. I wanted to save the company for her." He paused and looked down at his hands, his tone changing, calming. "No one wants to leave a failing company to their child. She still had more money than she knew what to do with."

I didn't know if I could trust a damned thing he was

saying, but I hoped that it was true. It didn't make it better, but there was something understandable about a father fucking up because he wanted what was best for his kid.

"That's not up for you to decide, though. It never was. As for me, I love your daughter, and I love our child. And if you want to be in either of their lives, you had better start changing your ways, because she might be willing to put up with it to the point where she's sick, but I'm not. I'm not going to let you hurt her ever again."

Her father sighed, his shoulders slumping as if he had been defeated. "I'm not leaving here until I see my girl."

"I'll take you back if you can act like a father long enough to check on her. If not, I'm going to throw your ass out of here myself. You don't have to like me or what I do, but I love your daughter, and I plan on taking care of her and my child. So you can either like it or not. It doesn't really matter to me."

I turned and started away, but he didn't move. I glanced back. "Are you coming?"

He gave a nod and followed. On our way, I explained that they were moving her up to a room and how she was going to have to stay for observation. "We're still not out of the woods," I said. "So, let's pretend we get along. For her and the baby."

I didn't wait for him to agree. Instead, I walked on down to her room, and we both went inside to find the nurse leaving. "She's resting. So don't you two wake her up. She needs that sleep."

I walked over and sat in the chair while her father looked down at her. It seemed as if he wanted to touch her arm, to stroke her in some comforting way, but instead, he took his hand away. He shot me daggers, still stewing about what had happened.

"When she was a little girl, I used to bring her up to the office and let her look out the window. Back then, she dreamed of working for the company. I would take her into my father's office and put her in his chair. Spin her around. She loved it. I knew then I wanted to give it all to her. That it was all going to be hers. My sister, Mary, she didn't have any kids. And so there wasn't anyone else to battle for the top position."

"That sounds like a nice dream for you. But things change."

"My dream was to have my daughter working there with me. That's why I've been on her to come back to New York and take Mary's place. I wanted to have time to show her the business." His shoulders moved as he exhaled a deep breath. "You'll see what I mean. Just wait until that baby comes. You'll realize what all you'll do for it. Lie, cheat, steal, all for their best interest. I just wanted to put the money where it would help her. I've done the same with my own."

"Well, we'll see. Her lawyer is going to have it investigated. She'll figure it all out."

He gave a nod, seeming to finally understand that he didn't have a choice in the matter. "I'm going to leave my address and phone number for where I'm staying. When you find out what's going on with her, would you please call?"

I nodded. "Sure." I wasn't going to tell him no. I was going to treat him with the same respect that I demanded he give me, as long as he was doing something to earn it. Not screaming at his daughter was a start.

He turned to look at me and said something that I was pretty sure gave him great pain to do so. "And thank you, Chris. Thanks for being there for my little girl when I couldn't be." He looked down at her and then turned around and walked out the door, closing it quietly behind him.

Fat tears rolled down Hope's cheeks. She had been listening the entire time. I didn't say anything to let her know I noticed. I just let her lie there calmly and deal with whatever she was feeling. As long as she was calm, she would be okay.

I sat there for hours with her, calling Nicole and Puck, letting them know what happened, and that we wouldn't make it out with them that night. And after dinner, which wasn't bad for hospital food, I walked down the hall to the waiting room to look out the window and talk to my mother.

"He claims he did it to save his company," I told her. "I think he was sincere. He said he did it for her. To protect her future."

My mother huffed. "That's mighty big of him. So, I guess he won't care if she seizes control of the company. If she keeps that lawsuit, which I filed today, by the way, then she just might be able to."

"I'm not sure she'll go through with it. I think she's just angry at the moment. I know she heard him. She was crying. I'm afraid she'll let him worm his way back into her life, and I'm not sure I want that for my baby."

"Well, just give it a little time, son. It's her father, and things get tricky when it comes to family."

I knew my mother was right, and while I hoped there would come a day when Hope would repair things with her father, I couldn't help but hope that she took her time. Deep wounds didn't heal overnight.

CHAPTER 26

HOPE

After my stay in the hospital was over, I went back to Chris's apartment, where Puck was working on a very special client. When he looked up, pausing his needle, he smiled. "Busted," he said.

Nicole looked up from where she lay, getting her shoulder piece tattooed. "Oh, you're out already?"

"You're actually letting him do it?" I said. "You must really like him."

Puck waggled his brows. "What can I say? I'm just a loveable guy." Nicole gave him a nudge.

"How are you feeling, mama? Did you get rehydrated? My little God baby was thirsty."

"Yeah, I think it showed its temper. It didn't like me being stressed."

"Neither did I," Chris said.

"So, did everything work out with your old man?" Puck asked, earning a look from Nicole.

Chris spoke up. "Well, I didn't punch him, if that's what you mean. I called him and let him know she was discharged and that we were on our way here. I wasn't about to bring her to her house."

I gave a chuckle as my phone rang. Chris was so sexy when he was being protective. "It's Virginia." I answered. "Hello?" It really wasn't a good time, but I was hoping this was about a sale.

"Hello, Hope. I was just calling to tell you that the man, the one interested in the painting, he's called back."

"He did? That's great." I breathed a sigh of relief. "And did he sound interested?"

"I told him to call you, but he said no. He's made an offer. It's twenty-five grand, but I wasn't sure if that was okay with Christian."

"Twenty-five?" I said aloud, looking at him. "And that would free up some space for him, right?"

"Of course," she said.

Chris nodded. "Tell her to take it!"

"We'll take it." I felt a rush of excitement. "Thank you for calling me, Virginia. We'll be in soon to settle."

I ended the call, and Chris wrapped me in his arms. "I'm so glad it sold." He spun me around, and then when I found my feet, I held on to him until I was steady.

"And you get the space added to your other space, so you had better get busy." He had a lot more walls to fill.

He took a step back and looked me up and down. "I'm feeling inspired already." We kissed until Puck cleared his throat.

"Some of us are trying to work here, man." He made a face.

Nicole giggled. "Yeah, so if it's not too much trouble, could you like, get out of here or something? You know, get a room?"

Chris held me close and pressed his cheek against mine. "You're just jealous because we're the cuter couple."

About that time, as the two of them protested, the door opened, and I was shocked to see my father walk into the shop. He looked older, and more surprisingly, contrite. "Hello," he said hesitantly. "Is it okay if I come in and talk?" Chris stepped forward, but my father held his hand up. "I just want to talk like adults. Calmly."

Chris shook my father's hand. "Let's go up to my apartment," he said.

My father glanced over and narrowed his eyes. "Nicole?"

"Yes, Mr. Mayhew, it's me. Don't worry, this tattoo is mom-approved." She gave a snicker, and then Puck went back to work.

"Carry on," my father said, walking up the stairs behind us. "You don't have any tattoos, do you?"

I turned and smiled at my dad. "Not yet."

"Not on her life," Chris said, overhearing. "I've told her she's perfect as she is."

"Well, at least we agree on that."

I rolled my eyes. "Don't start getting along just to team up against me." I walked into the apartment as my father followed. And while I sat down on the couch, he looked around the room.

"This is quite an old building," he said, walking around the room.

"It's historic," Chris said. "And I own it. My studio is upstairs in the loft. It's where I create my art."

"One of his paintings just sold for twenty-five grand. I just got the call, and since I'm his agent, I'll get a nice commission." It was nice sharing a bit of good news with my father, even if it was to rub his nose in the fact that Chris was making good money with his art.

Chris chuckled. "And don't forget to pay yourself the modeling fee." I knew he had only said that for my father's sake. And it worked.

"That's real nice," he said. "I wanted to talk to you about something. I've made a decision, and I want your opinion, as well as your blessing." I couldn't imagine what he'd want my blessing for. Other than turning himself in for stealing my money.

"I thought you might want to start with forgiveness," I said.

"Of course," he said, walking over to the couch. He remained standing. "I hoped that what I had to tell you might show you where my heart is."

"I know where your heart is, Dad. The same place you put my money. It always has been." Even he couldn't argue with that. I'd known it as gospel my entire life.

"Well, I thought that we could talk about that too." He seemed a bit annoyed, and I kept waiting for him to lose his temper. To his credit, he didn't.

"It's okay. I heard what you said in the hospital. How you wanted to leave me something. I understand wanting the best for your children. But you took it too far."

"Can you ever forgive me?" He gave me a pleading look. "I really did it for your own good. I realize now, I was wrong. It's just, I did the same with some of my money, and well, I considered it an investment. Besides, it helped keep the company afloat through some hard times."

"But it wasn't a loan. You didn't ask for it. And you sure as hell didn't pay it back."

"I know," he said, his head hanging low. "Again, I was wrong, and I apologize." My father almost appeared small when he was docile, and I wondered if that's why he felt the need to pound fists and be angry all the time.

There was still so much I had to learn about what made him tick. "I *can* forgive you. It's just going to take time." And that was the best I could do.

"Well, I anticipated that," my father said. "That's why I decided, with your blessing, of course, to buy a place here so I could be a little closer to my grandchild."

Hearing that warmed my heart, but it also scared me. I couldn't handle him being hard on my child as he was me. I'd murder him. "You hate Chicago," I said, not thinking he was serious.

But his next words shocked me. "I could learn to love it. Besides, my family is here. If you'll still have me."

Chris glanced up at me. "What do you think?" I asked him. I was really on the fence. If it was going to cause trouble with Chris and me and ruin the life we were creating together, I didn't want him anywhere near us.

"We only get one dad in life, Hope. I guess if mine was still around, no matter what he'd done, I'd give him a second chance. Besides, it would be kind of sad if the baby didn't know its grandfather."

"As long as we can get along, I guess it's okay," I said. "But I'm not coming to New York, and I'm not working for the company. I'm going to remain Chris's agent, and whatever else *I* decide to be. I called Paddy's and put in my two-weeks' notice. And I'm finishing school, and then I think I'm going to take another art class just for the fun of it."

That last part earned a smile from Chris.

"Sounds like you have your life all figured out." My father didn't look too impressed, but whatever was in his mind, he kept to himself for a change.

But I didn't want to do that. He had to understand

where I was coming from. "I've had it figured out, Dad. I've known for a long time that I would have to find my own way and make my own path. It's just new to you. But you had better get used to it. I call my own shots, not you."

"Fair enough." He sat there a minute, and after the pause became awkward, he glanced down at his phone. "I guess I should run. I have some business to take care of in town, but I'll get with you about dinner one night, and maybe you can help me find a nice apartment."

"I'll ask my realtor," Chris offered. "I'm sure she's got a few places."

Dad smiled a tight smile. "I'd appreciate that."

I wasn't sure how sincere he was, but I was willing to just appreciate the two of them being civil to one another. The rest we'd figure out in time.

Just when I thought it couldn't get any better, my phone pinged. It was the tone that I used for notifications from my bank account. When I glanced at the bank app, my heart nearly dropped to the floor. "Oh no, there's a problem with the bank. I better call them."

"There's not a problem," my father said. "It's *your* money. The money I took to put into the family business. I decided to give it back. I know it doesn't change what I did, and I understand if you still want to take legal action. If you ever want to invest, it's your decision, and besides, with the baby coming—well, let's just say that I know how expensive they can be."

My heart was so full of joy that I could barely contain myself. I walked over and hugged my father, who froze for a moment before putting his arms around me. "Thank you, Dad."

He looked into my eyes, and I saw the man I hadn't seen since my mother died. "I love you, Dumplin'." He squeezed me tightly. "I can't promise I'll be perfect, but I'll do better. I promise you that."

"That's all any of us can do, Dad, is our best. And I'm going to do what's best for my family too."

"Well, you did okay with Chris. Even if he is an artist." He made a face.

"Thanks a lot," Chris said with a chuckle.

"You're a good man. And I guess it doesn't matter if you don't have a *real* job. At least my daughter can take care of herself."

"Dad," I said, feeling embarrassed.

"He's only teasing," Chris said, giving him a pointed look. "Aren't you, Mr. Mayhew?"

Dad shrugged. "Oh, sure." He glanced at his phone. "I'm sorry. I must be going. I have an appointment. I can't be late." He hugged me one more time and hurried out after shaking Chris's hand.

"Well, that was unexpected," he said as he shut the door behind my dad. "I'm glad it's working out."

"Me too. Now, it's time to relax."

Chris looked at his phone after it pinged. "That's Puck. He said that Nicole and him are bringing up some food, so we had better not get naked."

"Why are we their friends?" I asked in a teasing tone. "They tell us to get a room, and now they want to come up? And just when we got rid of the old man."

"That's why we need to get our own place."

I couldn't agree more. I moved down on the couch, and we spent what little time before they arrived kissing. It was the little moments that we stole that meant the most.

CHAPTER 27

CHRIS

As Hope and I followed the realtor through the house, I was impressed by how much she knew about what she wanted and what she didn't. All I had asked for was an extra room for a studio, but she wanted us to have our own offices as well, and of course, we needed a nice nursery, located close to the bedroom.

Now that things were on the mend with her father, I felt like Hope had a better outlook on life. She had always been positive, but now it seemed more effortless as if her confidence had soared.

"What if we shared an office space, and then we could turn one of the rooms into a home gym?" I thought I'd been far too quiet, so I mostly said it for something to say. I could always work out in the attic or the basement. Or even the garage.

But Hope seemed to like the idea. "That's really a good idea. Could we do that at this price point?" I asked Carla, our realtor, who my mother had recommended.

She nodded. "You have enough in the budget for that,

considering you'd still have the same amount of rooms. And then, don't forget about the basement and attic space in this house. It could be converted to anything you want."

"I like the idea of an attic studio," I said. "Better light than in a basement, but I wouldn't mind turning the basement into a home gym. If you're down for that." I didn't really care so much about it; I just needed a place to work, and the rest was all to make her happy.

"I like that. But we need a bigger kitchen than this. I want to entertain, and this feels a bit like we're in a servants' kitchen."

"It is a bit removed," Carla agreed. "I have one more house I can show you. I have to warn you, the location is a little farther out from the city, but it is a newer neighborhood and about sixty grand over your budget."

Hope paled. She had wanted to keep things practical, despite the amount of money she had come into. Her philosophy was making it last and spending more quality time with the family instead of working. But I don't think she realized just how much money she had to play with. If her father's abuse did anything, it taught her to appreciate a dollar.

"We should at least look at it, right? Make an offer?" I could tell she was looking at me for what to do.

"I think so. Especially if we're planning on this being the first and last house we ever buy." That had been her idea. "We have a little wiggle room. I'll just have to sell more paintings." I winked at her, and she smiled.

"Yes, we'd like to see it, thank you."

As Carla made a phone call, she walked over and joined me at the window. "Do you like this one?"

"It's big and fancy, but it's also closed off, and there

aren't any walls that could be knocked out to make this an open concept."

"Yeah, I don't want to do that kind of work." She laid her head on my shoulder. "And I found out that my father's place is just down the road. It's in the big complex we passed on the way in." She made a face. "I mean, things are going good so far, but I don't want to live up his ass."

"Me neither," I said. "Then we definitely need to see the other house."

"Yeah, I mean, I dropped the cases against him since he gave me the money back, but I just want us to have our own space." She let out a sigh. "But it's so much more."

"And this is a *house*, Hope. Not a rental. It's ours. It's going to be our *home*, where we'll raise a family. I don't think we need to be bargain shopping. Especially when we can afford it. I'm going to keep working, and I know we'll be able to do this and still have the kind of life we want."

She kissed my cheek. "You're right. And I've been thinking about the money from the sale of that art piece. I want to start a savings account for the baby with my part of it. It's how we met, so I wanted the money to go to something special, you know?"

"I like that, but if you do that, then it's only fair I put my earnings in as well. It would be a nice start for his or her future."

"I like that." She turned when Carla came back into the room. "Can we see it?"

"Yes, ma'am. We'll head on over." Carla walked us to the door and locked up behind us.

We left the house and then followed her to the other location, and I was pleased with how far away from her father it was, but not so much the commute to the city. "We may as well say we're moving to the country."

"I've always wanted to live out this way. We will have a bigger yard, you know? We could build a playground for the baby when it gets older."

"I suppose. I'll be farther away from the gallery."

"It's not even ten minutes from the last house."

"It's eleven," I said, looking at the time.

She let out a sigh and rolled her eyes at me, but then, as the realtor up ahead slowed her car and turned into a long and winding path, Hope's mouth fell open. "It's gorgeous."

The dreamy look in her eyes told me that we had found our home. "It's really nice." The style of home was a bit different, but it had much cleaner lines, like that of a much older house.

When we stopped out front, Hope wasted no time getting out of the car. She walked over and stepped up on the porch. "It has a porch," she said. There was a swing out front. "I've always wanted a porch."

"There's one on the back too. The family who built this place a few years ago modeled it after their grandmother's Southern farmhouse, but inside, it's the open concept you were looking for. There are the same number of bedrooms, and you have the basement which has been fully water-proofed. It's almost an acre of land, fully fenced, and a three-car garage, in case you want to use part of it for a shop or studio."

"What about the attic space?" I wanted a lot of light and room for my art.

"I'm afraid it's not really that big. But I know it has something you'd like. Let's go inside." She walked up to the door and unlocked it. Then she opened the door and waited as we went inside.

While I wasn't expecting to have the aha moment Hope had, I liked what I saw.

She went straight to the kitchen, which had a big island and an even bigger bar. There was a breakfast nook that looked out across the lawn, and the previous owners had planted roses all along the windows.

"It's perfect," she said. "I can see us here."

I could see us there too. Not only could I see us, but our friends, our children.

"And, since I knew you wanted a nice place to make a studio, I thought this would be perfect," said Carla, waving us to the back. "Instead of being cooped up in some stuffy upstairs attic studio, how about this?" She opened the door to a room where the sunlight was so bright, my first thought was that half of the wall was missing.

"It's a sunroom," Hope said. Two of the outside walls were glass, as well as part of the ceiling.

"It was actually built as an atrium and sunroom, and as you can see, with it being an extension away from the top floor, you get the lovely skylight effect."

"It would be perfect," Hope said. "You would be able to do all of your painting, and you would have enough room to make a sitting area in case you want the baby and me to come in and sit with you."

I walked around, looking at the windows. I could see it with plants and my easels and a brand-new workbench with my paints organized along with my brushes. "I'll have to have a cabinet put in, and I'd need a sink. Someplace to wash up brushes."

"There's a half bath right there," she said, pointing to the hallway. "And that wall there would support cabinets for your supplies."

"Could we see the upstairs?" Hope walked out of the room with a smile from ear to ear as she glanced back at me.

"You'll love the master suite. There are two walk-in

closets, one for each of you, and a connecting office, and a connecting sitting room, which you could use for a nursery if you would prefer. There's a guest room down the hall, and another bedroom, with the fourth and final bedroom up in the attic space. That's why it was so small. But you could use it for a studio if you want."

"No, I'll take the sunroom," I said. I was already feeling inspired just seeing my life playing out in my head living in that home.

While the ladies went on about the closets, I walked back down to look at the studio. I took the measuring tape Hope had insisted I bring from my pocket and ran it along the floor where I wanted the cabinets to go. I needed countertop space as well.

Then it hit me. I needed Hope to like the house as much as I did.

About that time, she walked into the room. "I thought I'd find you here. It looks like you've found your studio."

"This room is great, but I can work anywhere. We have to live somewhere, Hope, and I want you to live in a house that you love. It's not just about the studio."

"I do love it. I mean, did you see that kitchen? I'm already cooking meals I've only seen on TV just looking at it. I can taste them."

As we shared a laugh, my phone rang, and I glanced down at it. "It's Virginia," I said. "I told her I was going to bring the last of the paintings tomorrow. She already has six. What more does she want, blood?"

I stepped over to answer the phone. "Hello, Virginia." I let out a sigh of frustration.

"I'm sorry to bother you. I tried to call Hope's number, but she didn't answer."

That's because she didn't want to be bothered. I should

have done the same. "Could I call you back? Hope and I are house hunting."

"Well, I thought you'd want to know that two of your paintings have offers."

"Already? We haven't hung them."

"Well, the client specifically asked for your paintings. They said they tried to get something of yours at the show but wanted a smaller piece. It seems you're not the only person infatuated with *The Pink-Haired Girl* series. And the two smallest have been inquired about twice already by another couple. They're supposed to come back at the end of the week."

"That's wonderful. I'll have Hope get in touch. Did you know which two it was?"

"*Eternal* and *Glee*. They loved the smiles."

"Perfect." I ended the call, doing the math in my head.

"Well? It sounds like good news."

"Two have interest. They are a serious buyer, and it's the two larger pieces."

"That's fifteen each. Thirty grand."

"It seems you not only inspire me, but you're developing a fan base. Two of the smaller ones have inquiries too. We're a success." I pulled her into my arms and held her tight. It was as if everything was going our way.

"So? What do you want to do?"

"What do *you* want to do?"

"I want to buy this house," she said. "And then I want to go and sell some art."

"Then that's what we should do." I pulled her close to kiss her. It didn't get much better than that.

As Carla walked back into the room, Hope said, "We'll take it."

HOPE

After a few negotiations back at Carla's office and settling on a price, I made arrangements for a substantial earnest money payment to get the ball rolling. Carla gave us a key, with the blessing of the previous homeowners to come and go as we pleased since the house was empty.

Once we left Carla's office, we got in the car, and I celebrated by giving him a big kiss. I didn't know anyone else I'd rather share that moment with in my life.

"I can't believe we bought a house," I said. "Can you?"

"I can't either. But I'm happy. You look happy." He held my face, stroking my cheek with his thumb. "I like that look on you."

"I do too. It's been crazy with my father, but I feel like I did the right thing. Don't you?"

"I think so. You certainly saved yourself from a lot of stress by not suing him. So, that alone was a very wise decision."

"I couldn't agree more. It's hard to believe now I let him get to me so much." He had wrecked the better part of my life, and worse, I had let him. "But it's time to move forward. If anything, maybe I can salvage a smidgen of a relationship with my father before it's too late."

"I like that. I'm glad it's working out."

"So, if I said he called me and wanted us to go by and see his new place, you'd be up for it?" I gave him a sideward look. "I mean, it's not until later, so we'd still have a little time to kill. Maybe grab some lunch?"

"I guess we could do that. But, as far as lunch, I've got a better idea." He started the car and then headed to the nearest deli. We ordered something to go, and then we got back in the car.

"So, that was your big plan?"

"Not quite," he said, starting the car again. "You'll see."

He drove out to the highway, and it wasn't until he took the exit to our new house that I realized where we were going.

"You want to eat our first meal there before the ink is dry?"

"It's already ours. So, why not?"

"I'm up for it. But I might have an idea of my own." I moved closer and put my hand on his thigh, and as I moved it further up his leg, I leaned over in my seat and kissed him.

"I like that idea too. Maybe we could christen every room?" He gave me a sly grin and then put the pedal down.

I giggled as we sped down the road, stroking his cock through his pants. He had to be as ready as I was. It had been days since our last time together because of how busy we'd been.

I had him so worked up by the time we got to the house

that once we got in the kitchen and dropped the food on the counter, he pulled me close and kissed me. The kiss lingered on for minutes, and then he picked me up. I wrapped my legs around his waist, and then he placed me up on that island in the kitchen that I loved so much.

"You want to do it right here?" I asked.

"Oh, yeah. Right here. So that every time I come in here, I remember." He moved in close and kissed me; then he pushed my skirt up my thighs as I reached for his belt.

It took me all of two seconds to have his pants around his waist. And less than that to have his hot, throbbing erection in my hand. My mouth watered, but before I could make a suggestion, he moved down, cupping my ass to lift me up a bit. Then he was between my legs, his finger pulling aside the fabric of my panties so he could give his tongue access.

As he lapped at my sex, teasing and flicking the tender bud, which had swollen with desire, I let the feeling consume me, bringing me over the edge.

It wasn't until he pulled away that I slid down the island and stood close to him. "It's your turn," I said, dropping to my knees.

I licked his shaft, then twirled my tongue around his head as I worshipped it. He let out a long breath as he stroked my hair, resting his hand on my head and pumping his hips. I enjoyed giving him pleasure and continued a while longer until my knees were getting sore on the hard tile floor.

Finally, after giving me a warning, he came, but I wasn't about to lose one delicious drop of him. When I moved away, still licking my lips, he pulled me up on my feet, spinning me around to face the counter. "We're only getting started," he said, pushing up my skirt and tugging down my panties. "I've been missing my girl."

He ran his hand between my legs and gathered my juices, then stroked his cock and positioned himself between my legs, nudging his at my entrance. I gasped as he took me, sinking his cock deep, burying it into my depths, which had me panting and moaning.

His energy was contagious, and I gave it right back just as good as he gave it to me. And before I knew it, we were out of our clothes, and my back was against the living room wall.

He drove into me hard, kissing my nipples, his arms tight from holding me. "Don't stop," I said, feeling the pleasure of him grinding on my G-spot.

"Do you like that, baby?"

"Yes, I love it. And I love you too."

"I love you," he said. "You're my girl. Always my girl." He seemed lost in his words and rhythm, and before I knew it, we were on the move again. He carried me to the stairs and then turned around to sit down. Then he backed his way up a few steps and stretched out.

I straddled his lap, stroking his cock with my long, cold fingers.

"Ride me," he said.

I smiled and stood his cock up, then moved up to straddle it, inching my way down little by little, until his base stretched me wide, his flesh filling me deeply.

"God, you're so beautiful," he said, putting his hands on my waist. He moved me up and down, then cupped my breasts as I took over the action.

He moved forward, capturing my sensitive nipple, nibbling and teasing it until it was tight and hard like a little pebble.

I pinched his too, and he threw his head back and moaned. "You know I can't stand that," he said. "It's too intense." He chuckled, taking my wrists and holding my arms out. He still managed for his mouth to find my breasts, but when he sucked my nipple, giving it a hard pull, I nearly came right there on the spot.

"They're sensitive," I said with a giggle. He wasn't just sexy; he liked to play too. And we enjoyed our time on the stairs. But soon, it was time to move on.

Once we got to the top floor, he took me into our closets and propped me up on the cubbies to take me from behind again. It was hard and fast, just how I liked it.

And as I was lost in my own pleasure, screaming his name, he released, pouring deep inside of me.

I collapsed forward, trying to keep myself up with arms and legs like noodles. "That was intense," I said. "I don't know if I'll ever catch my breath."

He gave me a cocky grin. "Well, at least we broke the new house in."

"Let's just hope that the other couple doesn't back out on us for some weird reason."

"It would still be worth it. We'd have the memory of doing it in a stranger's house. Kinky either way." He gave a soft chuckle and then took my hand. "I think we should get down there and get out clothes, though."

"Good idea." I put my arms around his neck and kissed him, then took his hand, and we walked down the stairs together, the two of us glowing, our smiles beaming.

We found our clothes where we left them somewhere between the kitchen and the living room, and then while I finished putting on my shoes, he went for our food.

"At least I worked up an appetite," he said.

"Well, I hope it makes it up for what comes next." We

had to go see my father. I didn't want to pull a no-show while he was doing his best to get along with me.

"I know," he said, looking disappointed. "Let's go and get it over with."

We left the house, making sure we didn't leave anything behind, and by the time we got to my father's complex, my bladder was about to explode. Being pregnant had me peeing every other minute, it seemed.

When he opened the door, I greeted him with a kiss. "Hey, Dad. Can I use your bathroom? Pregnancy bladder."

He chuckled. "Your mother had the same problem. She knew where every clean bathroom was in New York. Down the hall to the left."

I hurried in and took care of business, and when I walked back out, I could tell that there was something the matter with Chris.

My father had already poured himself a drink and was standing quietly near the bar that separated the kitchen from the rest of the main room. "Is everything okay?" I said, looking up at Chris.

"It's fine." He looked away toward the living room as if seeing something there he didn't like.

I walked over to where he stood and then turned around to see his painting of me, the eighteen- canvas masterpiece that now took up the entire wall on the other side of the room.

"I thought you might be happy," he said. "I bought it as a sign of goodwill. It's a fabulous work of art, and well, you captured my daughter's features perfectly."

I knew why Chris was upset, and that was because it felt a hell of a lot like a pity purchase. And while I wasn't sure why my father thought it was a good idea to have a larger-than-life painting of me and Chicago in his living room, I hoped he had done it to be nice and not to try and posture over my boyfriend.

"You were the mystery buyer," I said. "That's why you preferred to talk to Virginia."

"I asked her to keep my name private. I was going to hang it in the office back home, but I thought it would look better here."

I took a deep breath. "Well, it does look fabulous here." I wasn't going to let it get me down. Despite his motives, it had helped us. "And you should know that the money went to a good cause. We've decided to start a savings account for the baby."

"That's wonderful," he said.

Chris took a deep breath and stuck out his hand. "Thank you, and I'm glad you like it," he said.

We only stayed a few more minutes before we had to leave, and while Chris didn't say much on the way home, I knew my father had stolen his thunder.

"I'm sorry about my dad. He should have said something about the painting." I leaned my head against the cool glass of the window.

Chris shook his head. "It's fine. It's just, it was our thing, you know? The first big accomplishment we made together, and now he owns it. I mean, I really thought I had a fan base. Turns out, it was just your father's charity."

"I know what you mean, and I can see why it's upsetting, but look at it this way, we can see the painting anytime we want to, and we didn't need the money. Instead, it's going to his grandchild." I had to stay positive for a change. And besides, it was his turn to freak out. "I'm sorry."

He gave a growl. "Don't go getting upset and stop apologizing for him. Forget about it, okay? And you're right. If I want to see it, I'll just go pay him a visit. And on the bright side, one day, our baby will be able to see it in person and know that it was the painting I did when I first fell in love with you." He reached over and took my hand, holding it on the console, and we drove back across the city.

CHAPTER 29

CHRIS

I t didn't take me long to get over her father's power play. Hope could think it was whatever, but I knew the timing of it was a little suspicious, not to mention the fact that he'd kept it a secret.

What upset me the most was the fact that he had probably done it as if he was doing me some huge favor, just to show me he was capable of buying me. It didn't sit with me at all, but I was going to do all I could to make sure that I didn't let it upset Hope.

It was time to put it behind me. Besides, I had bigger things in mind.

So, by the end of the next week, when I had finished the final touches on my paintings and delivered them to the studio, I had my plans all set.

The only problem was I had to keep her distracted.

"That one doesn't go there," Virginia said. "I want the smaller ones along this wall and the medium to larger there." She pointed across the room.

"Okay," I said, walking the painting to the other wall, where the hanger had already been placed.

"I liked it better on the other side," Hope said. "The composition is too much like this one to hang it right next to it."

"You've got a point," Virginia agreed, scowling at the wall. "Put them back the way they were." She gave her order and then stormed off to the office where the phone was ringing.

"I told her no more anonymous sales. I don't need their personal details, but I do need their names."

"Look, Hope, I'm over it. I actually wanted to see if you wanted to go back to the new house for a bit."

"Sure. I do need to measure the front window. I think I've found the perfect curtains. If I order them now, they'll be here in time for the closing."

I smiled, not letting on that anything was out of the ordinary.

Once we finished with the placement of the pieces, which I was surprised Virginia let us help with, we left the gallery and drove across town.

On the way in the car, Hope fidgeted with her phone. "I can't get Nicole to pick up. Have you heard from Puck? Are they together again?" She rolled her eyes. "They are worse than we are."

"They survived their first fight, so you know it's serious."

"I still think he was being an ass," she mumbled.

"And I'm not getting it into it with you about them," I said, refusing to ruin the night by telling her how much I disagreed. Whatever happened, it was both of them being stupid and not our problem.

She gave me a look. "You know I like Puck, right? And I do think he'll be amazing for Nicole."

"I'm glad we agree."

"Why did you want to go to the house?" she asked me. It was the one question I had hoped to avoid. I wasn't good at lying, especially to Hope, so I decided I had better just play it cool.

"I wanted to take another measurement for the studio." I tried to sound as nonchalant as I could but then decided to change the subject. "Boy or girl?"

"Girl," she said. "At least right now. I like the name Paisley, but I think it might be a bit too common these days. I wanted something different."

"I'm sure it will come to you," I said. "I'm naming the boy." I still wanted my son. It had become a game for us to talk about our plans for each, the only rule being whatever she chose first, I had to choose the opposite. She had made up the rules, and while they weren't fair, it did give me a chance to daydream about having a daughter now and then. It wasn't that I didn't want a little Hope. But I was terrified to have a daughter. Little boys didn't scare me nearly as bad.

"I don't see why you want a little boy," she said. "You'd be so amazing with a little girl. She would be the apple of your eye; I just know it. And every bit of inspiration you feel from me, you'd have tenfold with her."

"Probably. But as long as she's just like you, I'm good." I wondered what having a little mini-me would be like, and then wondered what would happen if I had a daughter just like me instead. *Oh, Lord, help me.*

We drove on, making small talk, and when I got to the house, I could see the kitchen light on, just like I'd asked. I'd kept a close eye on my phone and had the all-clear five minutes earlier to let me know that things were in place.

"Oh no, did we leave that light on when we came by the other day?" She narrowed her eyes. "That's weird."

"No, I checked."

She looked concerned, so I needed to do something to make her relax. "It was probably Carla. She had to come and get her signs and the staging props." I was quick on my feet to think of that excuse.

"She hesitated to get out, but I walked around and opened her door for her. "Do you think someone's inside?"

"No, it's fine. Come on."

I took her hand and then walked her to the front door. When we walked in, she looked down at the rose petals that had been scattered.

"What in the world?" It didn't take long to hit her. "Chris, did you do this?" She put on a big smile.

"Yes. I wanted to do something special for you."

"But the papers? It's not our house yet." She fell into my arms and then pulled away, still with the question in her eyes.

"Actually, it is. Well, just as soon as *you* sign the papers. I've already done my part, and well, I told Carla I needed the house for a few hours tonight, and she said that was fine. We could move in if we like. She said with a deposit like that, how could she resist. I didn't know you paid half upfront."

She shrugged, giving me a shy look. "I went back and gave her more. I was afraid about the extra sixty. I'm not used to having all that money, and this will help us pay it off sooner. The sooner, the better."

"I hope that you have the same attitude when you see what's going on upstairs."

She smiled, giving me a sly look, and then she turned and sprinted for the stairs.

"Be careful, baby. Don't slip on the petals!" I went after her, but she giggled the entire way up and didn't slow down until I caught up with her, grabbing her around the waist.

She was so busy laughing that she couldn't speak. When she finally caught her breath, she turned her head and saw the candles lining the room ahead. "Wow, you really went all out."

"I had a little help from my friends," I said. "You might know them."

"This is what those two have been up to?" she asked with laughter in her voice. "I guess Puck isn't so bad, after all."

"I thought you'd feel that way." She had been so hard on him, taking Nicole's side in the couple's fight. I had known better than to choose.

She walked into the master bedroom and found a pallet on the floor surrounded by roses and petals. Candles lined the room; all were lit, which was why I had to time it just right. I didn't want to burn her house down before it was officially ours.

"I love it," she said. "But what is the occasion? We've already celebrated the house."

"The occasion is this," I said, dropping to one knee. I took the ring out of my back pocket and then held it out for her. "I love you, Hope."

She put her hand to her heart. "I love you too." Her chin began to quiver.

"I want to spend the rest of my life with you, and while I know you already told me you wanted the same thing, I was hoping for something a little more official. So, will you marry me?"

She took a minute to catch her breath. Her eyes turned red as fat tears spilled from the corners. "Yes. I will." She fell into my arms, and I held her close, knowing that everything was officially right in my life.

"We can do whatever you want, but I'd really like to marry you before the baby gets here."

Her face lit with excitement. "We haven't wasted any time with anything else. Why should this be any different?"

I breathed a sigh of relief. It was good to know we were on the same page. "I was thinking Vegas. We could go, bring a couple of witnesses, then ditch them for a honeymoon wherever you want to go."

She hesitated a moment, making me wonder if I had misread things. I knew she loved me, but marriage was a big step, and I couldn't blame her if she wasn't sure she wanted to take it. She took a deep breath, and I worried that she hated the idea.

It was time to stand down on the idea. It was probably too much too soon. "We don't have to rush; we could wait, do a big wedding. It's your decision." I held out my hand to let her know that I was okay with whatever. "I figure you've probably been dreaming of your wedding day your entire life like most girls, and if you want the fairy tale, I'll give it to you."

"No, I have the fairy tale already. I'm with you. I want to do it as soon as possible. I don't want to wait until I'm too big to travel, and I want us to move into our house as husband and wife." She bounced on her heels a bit as if she could barely contain her excitement.

"That sounds like a good plan to me. I can't wait until you're my wife." I had never really thought about my wedding day before, but I knew that whatever it was, as long as she was there, it was going to be perfect.

We spent the night making love and sharing a special memory that would last a lifetime.

As I lay stretched out in Chris's studio, I rested my phone on my belly and looked at Instagram photos of our Vegas wedding while he painted his next masterpiece.

He loved his new studio and had bought me the purple plush chaise as a housewarming gift.

"Say it," he said.

"No, I'm not saying it again," I said with a giggle.

"Come on, Hope. Just once more." I hated it when he begged. Especially when he was standing barefoot in his undies, with no shirt, and paint splattered everywhere.

"Fine," I said, rolling my eyes. "Paint me like one of your French girls, Jack." I used my most proper English accent.

He chuckled. "It's still hot. And I find it kinky when you call me Jack."

"You're delusional and deranged. And I hope our little one doesn't come out like you."

"Two weeks ago, you *wanted* him to come out just like me, now you've changed your mind?"

"I'm enormous. I have the right to change my mind." My body had gotten so big; I wasn't comfortable in my skin. The only hope I had was that this was almost over now. I'd been having Braxton-Hicks contractions for nearly two weeks and one false alarm. If the baby didn't come soon, I was going to lose my mind.

"I think you mean you're a woman; you have the right to change your mind." He looked up from the canvas.

"No, I know what I said, and I know what I mean. My feet hurt, and I want this baby out of me."

"You're not enormous."

"Please, you don't even paint me anymore. That's probably why you've taken to turning the canvas away from me, so I can't see."

He gave a huff and spun it around, showing me the pink-haired pregnant girl in the painting. "It's beautiful. And this one, I'm keeping for myself."

"Only because you know it won't sell."

"Stop talking about the woman I love that way, or I'm going to come over there and tickle you until you pee."

I got up, my big belly leading, and once I was upright, I felt a sharp pain and then a big release. Water gushed to the floor from between my legs. "Chris?"

But I already had his attention. "Hold on, baby. Don't move or you'll slip." He came over and helped me around the puddle. Then he went for some paper towels and tossed them over the mess. "Come on, we'll get you cleaned up, and then we'll get to the hospital. You still have some time."

He had read every single book and all of the ways not to panic to be prepared for this moment so I wouldn't be stressed out.

I took his hand again, and he helped me to the downstairs bathroom. "Get cleaned up, and I'll get you a change of clothes and your bag."

"Thanks." I closed my eyes. "Are you sure I have time?" I felt another contraction, and it was not that long since the one that broke my water.

"Yeah, I'm sure. Tell me when a contraction comes, and we'll time them."

I nodded and tried to control my breathing as I got into the shower. I rinsed off, letting my chin-length hair fall limp.

By the time I was ready to get out, I had another contraction, and I cried out for Chris, who came to my side to assist and give me comfort.

He played it cool still, but I could tell that he was getting nervous. "Okay, we're going to get you out and get you dressed."

Thankfully, it didn't take him long to get me dressed and to the car, and when I got to the hospital, Puck and Nicole met us outside.

"We'll be right out here," she said.

"You've got this, mama bear," Puck said. Then he shook Chris's hand. "Let me know if you need anything. If you forgot anything, whatever you need."

"Thanks." Chris hugged his friend, and then Nicole came over to hug me.

"I can tell you're scared. It's going to be okay. You've got this. You're strong."

"Thanks," I said, wishing my mother was there, but thankful I had someone like Nicole in my life who cared.

Just as they were about to wheel me away, Chris's mother, Olivia, came running into the hallway. "Honey, how is she?"

"It's progressing faster than I thought."

"It's okay. You're here now. You did good, just let them take care of her." He was finding it tough to let anyone else take charge.

"I feel so helpless," he said as he hugged her neck. "I wish I could help her more."

"It's okay, babe," I said, taking his hand.

They wheeled me away, and just as I rounded the corner, I spotted my father running into the waiting room. Nicole walked over and pointed to me as I was stopped in my chair, and I waved at him, and he waved back, giving me a thumbs-up.

I began to cry, thinking that was exactly what my mother would have done. She would have given me a thumbs-up to let me know that I had it and that everything was going to be okay.

Things moved fast then, and before I knew it, I was in my delivery bed about to break Chris's hand as the doctor asked me for one more big push.

Chris's eyes were as big as saucers one minute, and his face paled as the doctor announced, "Congratulations, Mama and Papa. It's a girl."

I began to cry, knowing I would love that little one with all my heart for the rest of my days. She was soon placed on my chest, and I cuddled her the best I could. She was so tiny; I felt as if I might break her. But then I knew she was mine, and we'd been through a whole lot together already.

Chris had tears in his eyes, and the staff gave us a moment before swooping in to take her to be cleaned up.

"She's perfect," he said. "I told you that you're an artist. Did you see that masterpiece?" He gave a soft chuckle as he gripped my hand.

I was excited but exhausted, and soon after, once I was

cleaned up and all signs of delivery taken out of the room, Chris went out to see our family while I took a nap.

It wasn't long until he came back, and behind him, a nurse brought the baby.

"I thought you would want to see her a little. Everyone was making a fuss over her at the nursery." The nurse swaddled her in the little pink blanket from the hospital.

"Did everyone leave?" I asked Chris, who couldn't take his eyes off me and our baby.

"No. They want to see you and the baby first. Your dad can't wait to hold her. He said she's the spitting image of you."

The nurse who had come in with him brought the baby to me. "Here you go. Make sure to support her neck. She's probably going to want to eat soon too. So, I can come back in a little bit and help you with that. The chart said you will be nursing?"

"Yes, that's fine, thank you." She handed me the little bundle, and when I took her in my arms, I wanted to cry all over at the miracle I'd been given.

The nurse left us alone a minute, and I took his hand and looked up at him. "Thank you," I said. "For giving her to me."

"Thank you. You did all the work. I'm so proud of you."

I felt proud of myself. I looked back down at the little one, who did look an awful lot like my baby photos. But she had her daddy's lips, and I hoped his smile.

"What are we going to name her?" I said. "Nothing I've thought of seems to fit now that she's here."

"I know what you mean. I can't think of anything perfect enough for her."

"She's everything, isn't she?"

"Beauty and grace. Innocence and peace. Purity." He stroked her little tuft of hair with his fingertip.

"My mother's name was Grace. I hadn't really thought about it until you said that."

"I think that's a beautiful name."

"What about Grace Olivia? After both of our mothers?"

"Perfection." He smiled. "Grace Olivia Tate. My mother will be so excited."

"Hello, Gracie," I said. "Welcome to the world, little one." I put my finger in her hand, and she squeezed it tight.

Then we heard a knock on the door. "Is it safe to come in?" Puck asked.

"Yes, it's safe," Chris answered, and shook his hand as he came in, Olivia and Nicole nearly knocking him down to get inside the room. My father trailed in behind them, staying in the back.

"Oh, she's an angel," Olivia said. "What have you named her?" She put her hand to her chest. "Please tell me you didn't go with anything weird like Puck."

Puck cleared his throat. "I think they went with Puck-ette. At least that was my vote."

Chris walked over and took my hand. "You do the honors, honey. You did all the work."

"We're calling her Grace, after my mother. So, I'd like you to meet Grace Olivia Tate."

Chris's mother began to cry, and my father moved in a bit close to get a look. As Chris handed his mother the baby to hold, my dad moved in even closer.

"She's beautiful, Dumplin'. Boy, would your mother be proud of you and that baby. You've done well."

I felt myself tearing up inside, the tears flowing as I

reached for my dad. He leaned in, hugging me tightly. "I love you, Dad. Thank you for being here for me."

"Thanks for having me. I can't tell you how proud I am of you and the wife and mother you've turned out to be. You're a good daughter too, you know. I know I never said it enough, but it's true."

My father broke like a dam, his tears spilling out across his cheeks, and when he stood up to wipe his eyes, Chris handed him a tissue.

"How would you like to hold her, Grandpa?" Olivia offered Grace to my father, and for the first time in forever, he looked truly happy.

He took the little bundle and held her close. "She's just like her mother was. So small. Petite. She's going to be a wonderful baby." I had never seen my father so emotional, not since my mother had gone. In some way, I felt as if he had come full circle, and maybe having Gracie in his life, he could start over and be happier too.

We visited and passed the baby around for another hour, as she slept, and when she woke up, she was ready for a feeding.

"To think all it took for everyone to leave was for her to cry. I think I'm going to like having her around." He gave me a smile, then tapped Grace on the arm with his finger. "We're going to have to learn a signal. I'll have you crying on command in no time."

"I don't think you're going to have to worry about that." She had a little set of pipes when she got tuned up, and it was only beginning.

As I sat there nursing her, amazed by the miracle she was, I looked up at Chris and thought of how lucky I was. Not only had I married the most amazing man, but I'd had his baby, and started a family with him.

"What are you thinking?" he asked.

"Just how crazy life is. I mean, I worked so hard to have the life I wanted to have when I didn't even know what it was I really wanted. If I hadn't taken that job at Paddy's or put my foot down about living in Chicago, then I wouldn't have met you, and she wouldn't be here with us now. I can't imagine my life being anything else."

"Me too. I'm glad I met my muse and fell in love with her. And I'm so, so grateful that you loved me enough to give me this beautiful miracle." He leaned down and gave me a quick peck. "I love you, Hope."

My heart was so full of joy, and I was glad I'd stood my ground and created the best life for myself. Life was full twists and turns and maybe a little pain, but it was worth it.

I'd never want to be anywhere else.

The End